The Carpils

M.D Ley

Illustrated by
Priya Pamela Naidoo

For:
Leanu and Tamika

'HOPE is real!'

The Carpils

First Printing, 2019

(Print Version)

ISBN 978-0-620-84326-3

For bulk copies enquire:

www.MDLey.com

Table of Contents

I

There was a loud ***Thud!*** Diggles banged on the palace gate. "What do you want?" said the half sleepy guard with his silver makeshift helmet drooping down his face.
Diggles dressed in old threaded pants and vest brown in colour, with various instruments hanging from his hip. "I have to see the King," said Diggles in great urgency.
"Whatever the matter for?" said the guard still trying to straighten himself up.
"I have urgent news and no time to delay, let me in I say" insisted Diggles.
"Alright alright, try and keep it down!" said the Guard with annoyance.

The guard's name was Uni, more so because of the shape in which both his eyebrows met in the centre. A large-little man that struggled with every breathe trying to open the palace gate. His face turning a plum red with each movement he made.

Finally, Diggles was allowed into the palace walls. There weren't as many Carpils' within the walls of the palace, many were just standing around trying to look busy. Diggles was escorted by Uni or Uni by Diggles, either way, they were both headed to the same location that is to the main palace entrance. The palace wasn't a grand design, from the outside it looked like empty match-boxes placed one on top of the other and painted in white nail polish. You see the Carpils' are people just like us except for a few minor adjustments - they vary in size and by age. To mention a few average attributes, they about one inch tall by one inch wide, long ears, deep heavy-set eyes, large belly, and on each hand and foot, they have only four fingers and four toes. Their feet are really small given their plump size, however, it works for them often having their bellies swishing from side to side trying to maintain balance. Most of the older Carpils' wore long gowns as a mark of respect and the younger Carpils' wore tightly wrapped pants and snug jackets, they weren't as plump as the older Carpils' and looked rather ruddy. None of the Carpils' wore any shoes and just rambled around barefooted with their small feet.

Very intriguing yet profound, the Carpils' lived below the carpet just below the wooden floor deck within a cavity of four inches deep. How the Carpils' came to live under the carpet and aptly derived their name, will be answered later on. However, what's important is that Carpils' are very shy and live private lives never seen or heard.

Uni finally arriving at the palace gates, huffing and puffing knocked at the large front door "We are here to see the King," demanded Uni.

"Who is here to see King Mosesha?" asked a frustrated usher. "We are," said Uni.

Diggles retorted back "I am here to see King Mosesha on important news."

"So whom should I say is wanting to see the King?" requested the usher.

"You know me its Diggles," sounding very annoyed.

"I know it's you Diggles. But protocol is protocol and I'll have you know that there have been some spotting's of nasties around" said the usher.

Diggles responding "One can never be too careful, now please let me in!"

"Alright, alright hold onto your pants and follow me," said the Usher "And Uni you can stay here, don't let anyone in and look sharp." Uni tried standing up straight but his large belly prevented him from doing so.

Diggles and the usher made it through the cardboard walls of the palace. There were decorative paintings of old Carpils’ on the walls. There was a dusty musk smell that lingered through the corridors. The same smell that lingered across the whole village. Diggles tried to quicken his speed with the usher tagging behind trying his best to keep up. They approached a large boxed off area, very smartly decorated. There was a large cardboard table for dining. A wide open area for large gatherings or parties. There were white Christmas lights strung across the area. The Carpils’ were scavengers by nature, they would gladly accept gifts that protruded and fell through the carpet. The Christmas lights being one of them and brilliantly used to light up the palace and the village. They even had a simple power station for the whole kingdom and an abundance of batteries.

King Mosesha aged two hundred and eight years was sitting alone at the end of the large cardboard dining table, big enough to seat around fifty dinners, enjoying his favourite caterpillar stew. Chewing and crunching on the little hard rings, one could clearly hear the sound of him slurping up the slime, it leaked onto his long white beard which he picked up with his fingers and slurped it right up again. You could see he was enjoying his meal as he didn’t bother to look up as Diggles entered the room.
“King Mosesha, I have some urgent news!” professed Diggles with the usher only entering the room shortly after.

King Mosesha, lifted his head slightly and peeked at Diggles with one eye, then went back to sucking out more of the green-yellow gooey caterpillar slime. Diggles was losing his patience but he was in the presence of the king and needed to speak only when spoken to. King Mosesha welcomed Diggles to sit next to him and called upon the kitchen staff to bring an extra plate for Diggles to share in the delicious caterpillar. Diggles couldn't help his eyes falling on the caterpillar, as you see caterpillars are very rare and difficult buggers to catch they need to be caught and killed very quickly simply because they give off a terribly unpleasant smell that spoils the taste. Carpils' regular diet consists of flies, worms, small roaches' and other little bugs that find their way under the carpet.

"What important news do you have?" asked King Mosesha still trying to get some tricky slime out between the crevices of the hard rings.

"Well sire, as you have requested….. And I have been through our lands…." answered Diggles in-between crunchy bites of the stew.

"Come out with it then" retorted the king.

Diggles stopped eating and took a gulp of foamy sugary water "Sire I have found the GREEN!"

"THE GREEN!" the king now standing up with full attention. Placing his bottle top hat on and his needle stick firmly wrenched around his stubby four fingers with great anticipation. "Tell me more."

Diggles went onto to explain how he travelled outside the safety zone of the village into the forbidden areas. Where treacherous growths of mould and dust gathered. Diggles explained the dangers of his journey when night and day was dark and all that guided him was the ability to see in the dark. "Hideous creatures, out there sire," said Diggles "I dare not speak of them, still gives me chills." Giving the king a full account of the days and months that followed him to the edge of the carpet, the cold brick wall….. All of a sudden Diggles froze with fear, his whole body pulling stiff, fingers, toes, eyes, long nose was all stiff. With a swift whack from the king's needle, Diggles unfroze slowly, his face returning back to normal.

"The 'Green' sire, I saw long blades of green sticking through the wall," said Diggles.

"I knew it Diggles!" yelled the king with great excitement. "We must see Wisen at once!"

King Mosesha summoned the usher to prepare the coach at once completely ignoring the caterpillar feast that still lay half-eaten on the table. Diggles however, made sure to finish the rest of it.

The coach was an old unwanted wooden toy car with wheels, fully working just unwanted by the Thumpers, the people that live above the carpet. Many objects in working condition were often left misplaced or forgotten by the Thumpers. It would eventually fall through the seams of the carpet and into the Carpils' village. There was an abundance of differently shaped silver and bronze coins, which the Carpils' appreciated as they came in very handy for buildings and amour.

The coach was pulled by two well-trained large roaches', strings were tied across the roaches' heads from the back of their bodies and tied to the front end of the wooden car. The driver of the coach sat on the bonnet and sometimes the roof of the wooden car and controlled the roaches' direction by pulling on the strings. There were bits of mashed up worms dangled in front of the roaches, to keep them focused on the direction which the coach driver controlled. Roaches' were very dynamic and useful creatures to the Carpils', not only were they a source of transport and food but also used for buildings, farming, and sport. Disobedient and dirty are some roaches'.

The king's coach driver, Floop, a young, dashing, nervous fifteen-year-old Carpil, dressed in brown pants and a tight pullover jacket had a great ambition to one day race a roach in the 'Three-G Race' the *'Great Great Great Race'* of all races. The winner would be known as the victor. Glory and free meals but mostly the admiration of young Carpil girls earned the champion veneration within the village. Floop dared to dream big. Once Diggles and King Mosesha were tightly squeezed into the back seats of the wooden car coach, Floop grabbed the reigns and off they went to see Wisen the enigmatic mystical one. The keeper of the *'Ye'Ol Book'*. The journey would take approximately twenty-seven minutes from the main palace gates to the far edge of the village where Wisen lived. This allowed Diggles enough time to explain more of his journey to an intrigued King Mosesha.

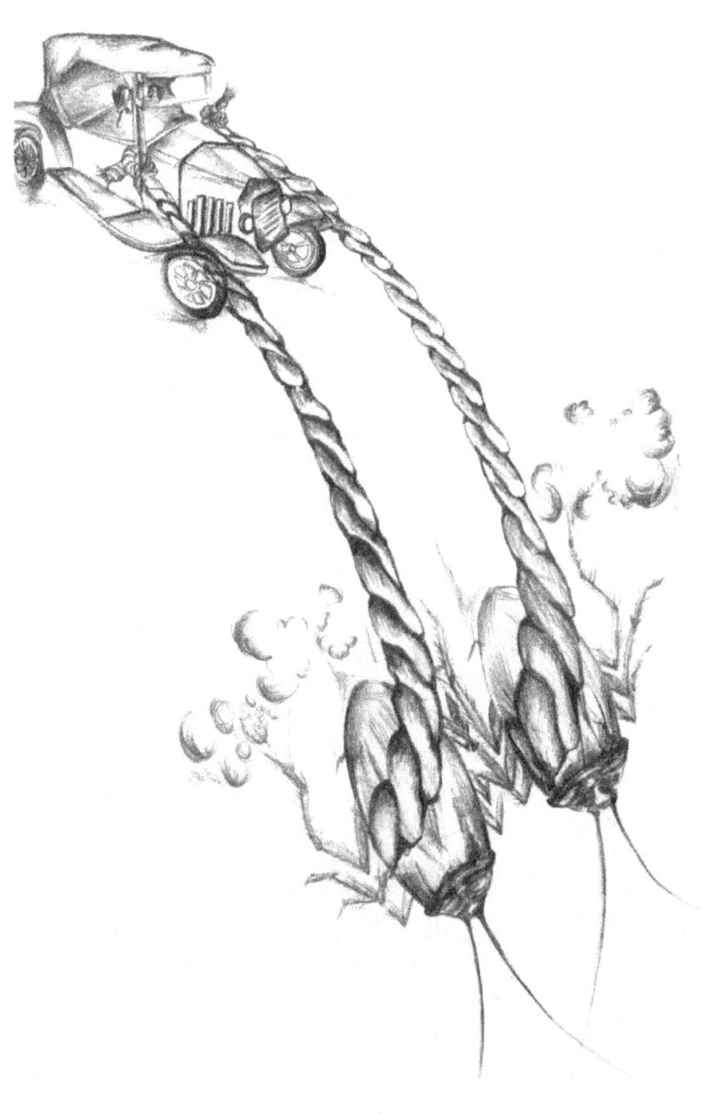

Diggles explained the unexplored territory beyond the village in great detail as a dangerous wasteland. Great high walls that surrounded the kingdom with large holes and wicked large creatures furry with two big front teeth and foul smelling breath about fifty times bigger than roaches'. Clumps and clumps of fur with pink long tails. King Mosesha wanted to know how Diggles managed to escape from the clutches of these beasts and survived the journey. Carpils' are very intelligent and resourceful and Diggles was such a Carpil. Diggles explained that he didn't know in the wasteland when it was night or day, there was no shimmer of light and the even the slightest light from his small torch would provoke and attract the unwanted creatures towards himself. Diggles continued to explain that even though he had good night vision, he still smelt like fresh meat and that was luring a lot of attention, especially from the furry beasts. He continued to explain that the only way to blend in and not to smell like a gourmet meal was to smother himself with the faeces of the furry beats. Yuck! King Mosesha took a huge sniff to ascertain if there was still any reminiscence of the smell on Diggles, a slight pungency tainted the air but Diggles assured him that he washed himself off through the water leak in the wall and with great eagerness continued his story. "So there I was, all smelly and dirty, still not knowing what time of day or night it was when something occurred to me, whenever the Thumpers stopped thumping all went still from above and that's when I realised it was then that the furry beasts came out to feed. I managed to find a crevice along the side of the wall and I squeezed myself into it, leaving just a slight space for me to peek from.

When the Thumpers started moving around from above I too started to move and I gained more ground. It was as though the Thumpers and I were doing a synchronized chromatic dance. The one thing I learned is that Thumpers make a lot of noise, there was a lot of gurgling sounds and shouting. I never understood a word or phrase that was being said but they scared the roaches' and furry creatures, so that did well by me."
King Mosesha interrupted Diggles "And when did you see the green?" he asked with excitement.
"I was getting to that sire" answered Diggles and continued his story.
During this time Floop was listening into the story and also persuaded Diggles to continue "So then what happened and what's the green?"

Diggles continued, "So there I was creeping alongside the walls firstly to avoid any more creatures and secondly, I knew the wall would lead me somewhere, I just didn't know where though. I moved gently and quietly when the Thumpers moved around I moved. I got lost in time and dates, I didn't know how many days or even months passed by. It was a cold, dark and miserable place. I could have very well been gone for three days, I don't know, but it felt like an eternity. Suddenly, I was caught off guard, perhaps I forgot to smear more faeces on me or just got lost in the time but just then out jumped the furry beast through a hole within the hole. I fumbled and fell between some rounded pebbles. The furry thing kept gnawing at me between the round pebbles. I managed to pull myself upright and started running. I ran as fast as my short legs would carry me, my belly swaying from side to side making me run in an unwanted zig-zag formation. It worked! As the furry beast lunged to take a bite out of me it missed and bashed into the wall. I was running so fast that at one stage I felt myself lift off the ground and felt as though I was flying, I think I was flying because I remember looking down and my feet were clearly off the ground and then *THUMP!* I had hit into the end of the wall where another wall formed. I thought it was the end. The furry creature lay over my body passed out, it must have also hit into the wall I assumed. Slowly, I managed to squirm my way from underneath the beast. I stood up and dusted myself off, slowly picking up my instruments as to not awaken the beast and placed them back into poaches on my side. It was then that I saw it. "Saw what?" yelled Floop from the top of the coach.
"The Green!" said Diggles gleefully.

Long strains of plush freshly smelling leafy green sticking through the wall. Mesmerised I was. I couldn't help myself and I touched it. It was soft, tender and slightly prickly but warm to the touch. I immersed myself in the green and lay there for a while. I was rudely disrupted by the sound of snarling. The beast had awoken. I didn't even have time to pick a sample all I could do was run for dear life and I ran. Eventually, I was out of the forbidden area but I still smelt of it. Quickly, I ran to the closest wall water stream I could find. It was just on the border of Petunia's home, the crazy old lady kept on screaming at me "get out, get out, you filthy roach!"
And that's when I made haste to see you, sire. "And it's a wise thing you did Diggles" responded King Mosesha.

II

In exactly twenty-seven minutes the coach pulled up at Wisen's home. Situated on the far outskirts of the village. Wisen was a very private and secretive man. The home was made out of old match sticks placed together as struts to support the house. It wasn't very well maintained as the front stick fence was falling apart, Floop tried his best to secure the roaches' to the dangling fence. With huge effort King Mosesha and Diggles managed to climb out of the wooden coach, often squeezing against each other. King Mosesha and Diggles were making their way towards Wisen's front door when Floop requested if he may join them as it was rather dark and dangerous. King Mosesha looked around the vast area and probably assumed Floop was a bit of a scared young chap and thought to himself what harm would it be and suggested Floop join them. All three of them, King Mosesha, Diggles and Floop made their way to Wisen's front door. King Mosesha used the top edge of his needle walking stick to knock at the door. There was no answer, again King Mosesha knocked at the door. Still no answer. As King Mosesha was about to knock a third time, the door lunged open and a wind swished passed them. Once the air cleared, to all three of their surprise in front of the door stood a young Carpil maiden around fifteen years old, dressed in a vest and tight leggings. She had the most beautiful brown eyes with her hair loosely braided behind her ears. Floop smitten quickly managed to push himself in front and nervously introduced himself,

"Hello I am Flock, I am Flip, I mean Floop."
The maiden simply giggled and responded "I am
Sena," thereafter moving her gaze
towards the King and clumsily giving a curtsy "King
Mosesha, sire please come in."

The home inside was very dusty with small glass
laying around on the table and tubes bubbling away,
small dusty books rested on shelves. The place smelt
of burnt rubber. Wisen appeared, dressed in a black
long gown which all presumed was probably white
before. Wisen was one hundred and eighty years old,
his face smudged with smoke, he had one large beady
eye and one normal eye, long slangy nose and a long
untidy white beard that touched the ground. Wisen- the
great keeper of knowledge and alchemist of the
village.
"Greetings, and what brings you here sire?" asked
Wisen
"The green!" responded the King.
"Wisen starring with his beady eye at the king "The
'Green' you say, what *hogwash*, the green doesn't
exist."
"It does, I saw with my own two eyes," said Diggles.
Wisen walking up to Diggles and inspecting his eyes,
poking and protruding it "The green?" asked Wisen
intrigued. "And where would one find this green?"
"At the edge of the wall, there it was," answered
Diggles.

Diggles went on to explain how he made his way find
to the green and drew out a map. Wisen listened
carefully and stared at the map for some time then
eventually leaned towards king Mosesha.
"So it's true, the green is still out there!" said Wisen.
"It seems that way" agreed on the King.
Wisen looking suspiciously at Diggles "Can we
believe this fool, do his eyes deceive him? We have
been tricked before!"
"I am no fool I might add, studied for many years on
the terrains and well educated in ecology" retorted
Diggles "I know what I saw, and swear upon the
'Ye'Ol Book' if have to."
"That you shall!" Yelled Wisen.
Wisen swiftly made his way to an old bookshelf and
pulled out a thick dusty book and placed it on the
table.
"This is the **_Ye'Ol Book_!**" professed Wisen. Floop and
Sena gasped in awe.
"Sena would you mind making our guests some lovely
hot wooden splinter brew, I have a story to tell."
requested Wisen.

Wooden splinter brew also called _'stick-beer'_ is made
from rare pieces of wood that fell from the roof of the
carpet into the village, musky in smell but once boiled
for exactly three and a half minutes no more, no less,
the sticks would disintegrate and form a foamy sweet
broth. This was the beverage of choice within the
Carpil kingdom and village. Sena carefully set the
stick-brew on the table. Wisen took a seat on an old
rickety wooden cardboard chair and started his story.

"'**This *Ye'Ol Book'*,** documents the history of the Carpils' and the time before we were known as Carpils'. From the very, very wise to the Kings before Kings, all is written in this book. You see many years ago we were known as Groundies. We all lived harmoniously within the green blanket that covered the earth. There were many foes and friends but we were once free to roam without limitations. We built homes and villages and most lived in peace within the kingdom of the green. We feasted on mushrooms, potatoes, flowers and other many sweet roots. These words may sound foreign to you Floop, and but that was before your time. Let me tell you more… there were beautifully coloured creatures that flew and crawled amongst us. There were streams of clear water and *squiggly* tadpoles that would swim ferociously through them. Oh, the fun we had. Times treated us well. There were no *Thumpers*, no roof above our heads, clear bright beautiful skies that adorned and shone brightly on all the green. The potions I would make were tremendously powerful, I had concocted a secret potion that would make any Groundies faster than any two or four-legged creature and that did well to outdo bad critters and nasties that tried to bamboozle us. There were many Groundies and villages spread across the vast green each with their own separate kingdoms yet we all lived in harmony. There were normal fights or arguments amongst villagers and other kingdoms but that was quickly and hastily resolved with a great feast. Groundies loved to feast, any excuse for a feast. Within our kingdom we were led by King Mosesha's father King Tate, however, King Tate had passed on at the exact age of two hundred and twelve. Groundies only live to a maximum age of two hundred and twelve years and exactly on their two hundred and twelfth birthday the light within would go out. We never really understood why but we all became accustomed to it. Planning for it suited us for we knew that when a Groundie turned two hundred and twelve they would have the chance to plan accordingly and to say their own final departure speech. With that came a celebration and a feast. It was never a sad or sombre occasion, a Groundies life was celebrated. After King Tate's light went out and the celebrations were over King Mosesha at the age of one hundred and thirty-six was crowned as the new King together with his wife and our Queen lady Pearl. Kings and Queens from other kingdoms were invited to partake in the crowning and the feast that followed. That was about seventy-two years ago. King Mosesha had a lovely daughter who would have been the only heir to the throne. Princess Shamora. King Mosesha and Queen Pearl ruled over our kingdom peacefully for the next twenty years. All was blissful and then suddenly fifty-two years ago large enormous metal beasts ripped through our Kingdom. There were screams and panic within the kingdom. Groundies were running in every direction seeking shelter. It was then that many Groundies were displaced including our beloved Queen and Princess."

"And then what happened?" interrupted Floop.

Wisen continued with the story despondently "Wooden planks were laid upon our area of the Kingdom- the green- and high walls built. There was another layer of planks laid and another softer dark material placed over the planks. The whole place went dark, luckily we had fairly good eyesight in the dark. The few of us Groundies were alone, cold and isolated. Everyone searched frantically for their loved ones, banging on the walls trying to jump onto the carpet, it was too high. Cries of despair lingered but not answered. As time faded and faces hung, King Mosesha called all the Groundies and said the following, ***"We should not despair and never give up, and we are Groundies strong, agile and smart. What happened has happened and cannot be changed. We have to deal with it now, we all have lost loved ones, and you and I have lost our Queen and Princess. We can only hope that all our loved ones are safe beyond these high walls and as long as we have hope in our hearts and no matter how long it takes we will continue the search. Hence, from this day forth until we are reunited with our fellow Groundies we shall be called the Carpils', for we dream of a day when we all shall again see the GREEN."*** There were cheers from all the now new Carpils'. Everyone gathered all the items they could find and started the rebuilding process. As years went by, us Carpils' learned to survive below the carpet, accepted any unwanted gifts that fell below the carpet from the *Thumpers*, changed our eating patterns from being purely herbivore to omnivorous eating any critters, bugs, worms that surrounded us. At first, they did taste very awful but with time and with a few ingredients and creative cooking we managed to master it. Many years went by

and the Carpils' began to build a new life with a new off-spring example, you Floop and Sena. It was then promised throughout the Kingdom never to mention the Green again as to not fill young Carpil minds with a fantasy world, a place that may never be found. The search did continue and many explorers failed and never returned. Until you Diggles."
"Hope!" King Mosesha cried.
Wisen drew in a deep breath and answered with a sigh "Hope."

Everyone had drunk their stick-beer accept Floop. He kept on staring at the map Diggles had earlier drawn out in amazement. His mind wandering. His eyes were immersed too deep into the map so much so that he could not hear the conversation that was taking place behind him.
"Floop" yelled Diggles "forget it, way too dangerous especially for a young Carpil like yourself.'
"Yes, the journey is very dangerous and we cannot risk any more lives," agreed the King "just knowing the green is out there is enough."
During this time Wisen had forgotten completely to introduce Sena.
"Everyone this is Sena my willing assistant and granddaughter of Petunia," said Wisen.
"The crazy lady?" responded Diggles "the lady that often shouts and screams around the village, saying we are not alone?"
"Ay that's my grandmother" retorted Sena.
Diggles humbly apologized. It made sense Petunia wasn't all that crazy there was truth in her outbursts. All went silent probably sharing the same thought.

"Well, what do we do?" asked Floop "carry on pretending that all is well and this is our only existence?"

"We have gotten by fairly well thus far" answered Wisen "sometimes living in oblivion is best."

"I don't agree" responded Sena, "I think we have a right to know, if something is out there bigger and better, the choice should be ours."

"Yes! The choice should be ours or at least be given the chance." agreed Floop.

There was an intense argument that followed. The older Carpils' mostly in disagreement while Floop and Sena argued their case. As the argument got heated between Diggles, the King and Wisen, Sena managed to grab a few glass bottles from Wisen's potion mixing station, Floop grabbed the map and both Sena and Floop slowly slipped away through the door. They untied the two roaches', jumped on them and rode away.

"It is decided!" Yelled the King "we shall never mention the *'GREEN'* ever again."

Wisen turned frantically looking around for Floop and Sena. "They're gone" he gasped. "What will become of them?"

"Looks like they took the two roaches' with them, we stuck here," said Diggles. "By the time we catch up with them, they would have already made into the forbidden land towards the green."

"Mmmm," said Wisen deep in thought "The way I see it, we have two options, the first being is to let them do this on their own or the second option is to return back to the village and regroup our best hunters to follow closely on their trail as reinforcements."

Sena rode with great speed and Floop followed her. He thought to himself that he may not have a chance of winning the 3-G Race if Sena entered the race. The thought quickly vanished as he caught up to Sena. "Where are we going" yelled Floop.
"To my grandmother Petunia, we need supplies" yelled Sena back.
Floop and Sena arrived at a lovely wooden pink house. Petunia took pride with her home and had painted it with the brightest pink nail polish that had ever fallen through the carpet. Floop and Sena tied up their roaches' and darted towards the house only to be accosted by Petunia.
"And where do think the two of you are off to?" Demanded Petunia "Off to get married like your mum and dad?"
Petunia aged ninety years largely built lady with full long grey hair dressed in a bright pink gown. She would have been thirty-eight years old when the green disappeared. It was almost impossible to squeeze around her to get away.
"It's not like that Gran" answered Sena "we would rather not talk about it, besides, we in a rush."
"Well young lady, you're not going anywhere, you with your big ideas," responded Petunia "sit down and tell gran what you're up to."

Sena and Floop were forced to sit on bright pink cushions. Everything was pink. Pink doorknobs, pink roof, and pink floor even the cutlery was pink. As it was Sena's grandmother, Floop decided that she shall do all the talking. Sena thought to herself that if she mentioned anything about the green to her gran, hysteria would break out and she and Floop would never be able to venture out looking for the green. Their adventure would stop right here and go no further. A single white lie wouldn't hurt, Sena thought to herself and the words just kept rolling off her tongue as Floop listened and watched in amazement. "You see gran," said Sena convincingly, "Do you remember when I was a little girl and not much like the other girls?"

"Do I remember, that's the reason why I painted the whole place pink, hoping that would influence you to become more ladylike!" responded Petunia.

Sena continued with her flamboyant white lie, "I have decided to follow in your footsteps and become more ladylike, the urgency you see is that I have managed to acquire a small piece of land not very far from you and close to the village. I have placed a peg in the ground and would want to start building a beautiful pink house much like yours. Therefore, I hired this fellow Floop as my builder, he comes with years of experience in the fine art of structural buildings and is in high demand. I have agreed to pay him his wage once the house is complete. I will take lodging at the old Canon house in the interim to keep a close eye on Floop. Now I must make haste before anyone else decides to outbid my peg in the ground. It shouldn't take more than a week or two so you need not worry as Floop has agreed to also cook for me. But I would need a few things from your kitchen and some clothes from my room."

"Well why didn't you say so in the first place, I am so proud of you," cried Petunia, "take what you need and need what you want, now make haste."

Sena packed up as much food and clothes as she could carry in a satchel. The rest she gave to Floop to carry along with the bottles of potion that she managed to grab from Wisen's home. They bid Petunia well and jumped back onto the roaches' and off they went. Sena and her fellow Carpil strutted on their way to the unknown.

A cloud of dust followed behind the roaches' as Sena and Floop rode towards the forbidden land. They finally approached the outskirts of kingdoms safety. They looked back and the distance between the safety zone and the forbidden land drew further and further apart. The road towards the forbidden land was filled with lots of unwanted objects that had fallen through the carpet, resembling that of a dump site. Floop stopped and dismounted his roach and ruffled through the objects. There were some peculiar objects that stared back at Floop and caught his attention. Besides Floop being the coach driver for the King, he also worked at the village power station and had a keen interest in the electronics that the Thumper's had willingly forgotten. Sena in the interim scouted around for empty bottles and various strange liquids. Both Sena and Floop continued searching in their own piece of terrain, totally oblivious to each other until a loud cluttering sound disturbed them.

"Who dares enter my dwelling?" came a voice from below the clutter.

A dirty, scruffy old Carpil man, dressed in tins, wires and rags, with his long dirty beard. Probably hadn't bathed in years. He reeked of rotten worm meat. Both Floop and Sena were immediately taken aback.

"We mean no harm, we're just passing by," responded Floop.

"Nobody ever comes here," said the man "this is the edge of the forbidden land."

"Just travellers, that's all," replied Floop.

"Travellers you say," yelled the man "this is my territory and if you want to pass you need to join me for dinner. Besides I don't get much company"

Floop looked at Sena for some consensus and agreement. Sena shaking her head in disapproval. "So be it, we will join you," responded Floop clearly ignoring Sena's gesture of disapproval
"Then it's done, follow me," suggested the man.
"Wait before we partake in your dinner, would you perhaps allow us to take a few items from your *wondrous* collection?" suggested Floop.
"Mmmm, *wakity takity*, perhaps we could come up with some arrangement," suggested the man. "Let me think!"
The man scratched his dirty scruffy beard. While looking around, a few tiny critters of unknown origin dropped from his beard to the floor and scuffled towards them. Sena jumped into Floop's' arms, which made Floop feel somewhat of a protector.
"Eeew!" screeched Sena in disgust.
"We may have a deal, those two roaches' over there," said the man.
"Yeah," answered Floop still holding onto Sena, however, slowly releasing his grip on her. "They're well trained they are."
"Well," said the man "seems as though we might have a deal then, you may take what you like and I would in return have those two roaches'."
Floop thought to himself that they wouldn't really need the roaches as they would travel by foot into the forbidden land. That would be a good deal especially if they wanted to get out of the area as soon as possible. Both of them grabbed from the piles of rubbish what they needed. Floop made sure to grab two small torches (miniature Christmas lights) and some extra batteries.
"Agreed!" responded Floop.

"Now follow me young-ins, let's have some dinner," said the man.

Floop and Sena followed the man keeping a good distance behind him. They approached an old open dirty and smelly area. There were tiny stones used as chairs. There were old fermented worms of all sizes hanging from the walls. Big worms, squeamish worms, fat worms, thin worms, fuzzy worms. The worms stank of an old fart.

The man suggested, "Please sit down I don't get many guests, I think I shall make you a lovely *inside-out* worm soup."

The man pulled down one of the worms and continued bashing it until it was all mush, then he placed it into an old pot adding some ingredients directly from the floor. It made Sena want to throw up. He continued stirring away and babbling on about how he has lived on his own for the past fifty-two years. Within his babbling and complaining, he made some reference to the days of the Groundies, although intrigued, Floop and Sena decided to be best not to engage in the conversation and sat still on the tiny pebbles regretting that the food was almost ready and they would have to partake in the meal. The man dipped his dirty fingers in the soup swirled them around and tasted it.

"Fantastic!" Cried the man. Dishing the foul worm soup into bowls and serving it to Floop and Sena.

"Eat up, come on now!"

Sena smelt the soup and gagged. Floop not wanting to create any altercations held his nose and swiftly gulped the soup down. His face *twitching and squirming.*

"Good isn't it," said the man.

Floop uncomfortably shaking his head in agreement.
The man suggesting to Sena that she try the soup. Sena
shook her head in refusal, seeing the annoyance and
persistence from the man, Floop took the bowl away
from Sena.
"She is not used to such a fine meal," said Floop
gulping down Sena's bowl of mushy *inside- out* worm
soup.
"You must stay the night." suggested the man.
"We don't mean to be rude and we are most thankful
for your hospitality, "replied Floop, but we must be
off, our parents are expecting us home."
"But I insist!" yelled the man whilst staring at Sena.
Sena kept still and silent all the while. Floop pondered
for a while. Then suggested they have a drink to good
times and willingly poured a few drinks. Floop *nudged*
Sena who was still sitting still and frozen.
Whispered Floop to Sena, "Do you have any sleeping
potions in your bag?"
"Yes, I do," Sena whispered back.
Sena pulled out a small bottle clearly marked
'Delirium' and poured some contents into the man's
drink. Floop suggested that they all have a celebratory
drink and handed the infused drink to the man.
"To good times and friends a merry," said Floop.
They all drank the prepared drinks, the man totally
oblivious to the contents of the drink slugged it down
and gave a huge burp.
"That's it we will wait for him to fall asleep and make
our exit," whispered Floop.
The ***'Delirium'*** worked faster than expected, within
two minutes the man lay flat passed out. It was time
for the escape. Sena suggested Floop take the roaches'
with them.

"A deal is a deal, we made a deal so the roaches' are his, besides we are not going to have use for them in the forbidden land,'" whispered Floop.
Both of them tiptoed slowly out of the smelly man's compound and headed back on route to the forbidden lands by foot. They had no idea what still waiting for them in the forbidden lands.

They reached the edge of the forbidden forest, it was easy to tell that the breeze that hit their faces, smelling of pure rot. There was an eerie feeling that could be felt in their bones, faces and toenails. There was an uneasy invisible strangling cloak that could be felt all around them. Sena suggested that they spend the night at the edge of the forest. They unpacked their items from their collection. Floop made sure to check that both small torches were working and Sena counted out all the potions that she had taken from Wisen. The potions perfectly labelled with descriptions *'Delirium'* - to make one delirious. *'Dew'* - to create smog. *'Splinter'* - to make one run fast. *'Lotus'* - to make one smell sweet. *'Flignog"* - to make one smell terrible. There were various other potions but those were the most important. Floop and Sena lay on mats not to close and too far from each other both individually and evenly spaced from one another. Both were in deep thought. Sena suggested the rest of the following day they should planning the strategy. Floop sensed that Sena was rather anxious and made small *chit chat* to distract her wandering mind.
"I know most of the villagers and it's strange that I have not met you," said Floop.

"I didn't go to the village school and was raised by my grandmother Petunia," responded Sena "would you like to hear my story?"
"Please."
"Well if you must insist," answered Sena.
"Please start at the beginning," requested Floop.
"The beginning?" Sena asked.
"Yes."
"The very beginning, I don't think I can remember from the very beginning. I can probably start from when I was six years old, I am fifteen years old now," responded Sena.
"I am fifteen too," said Floop in excitement.
"Are you going to allow me to continue?" asked Sena in exasperation.
"Continue, just saying it's a coincidence."

Sena continued with her story, "as I was saying, I was six years old, my parents and I lived in the village as normal Carpil folk. My mother worked at the *'Needle and Thread shop'* as a seamstress. My father, grandmother Petunias son worked as a general handyman for the villagers, he was rather good with his hands. I would accompany him as a child on every job he did. On one fateful day, a day that I wish could not have happened but it did. My father and I had decided to surprise mum by taking us all to the local theatre play for her birthday. It was a *wondrous* and fabulous play with non-stop laughter, we laughed and laughed till our bellies ached. We were walking home when I felt a big push and a scream that followed! My father had pushed me out of the way, by the time I turned around it was too late. A huge plank from the top of the carpet had fallen, both my parents never made it. I was then taken to live with my grandmother Petunia and grandfather Shroom. Overcome with shattering grief my grandfather Shroom ran off into the forbidden lands and has never returned since. It was just my gran Petunia and I. Over the following years I watched my grandmother go a wee bit *loopy*. She started painting everything pink, talking in riddles and mentioning the other side. She is of sane mind just goes *whoopsy* at times. I couldn't go to the village school as by then grandmother Petunia was commonly referred to as the lunatic lady. It was decided that I would attend school in an unusual way. Grandmother was friends with Wisen, I suppose he took pity on me and decided that he would teach me as his assistant or more like a prodigy to himself. I rather enjoyed it, it was isolated and fun. I was taught the fine art of alchemy, anatomy and biology. Though many a time I

almost blew up Wisen's house with the wrong potion mixtures. Well, that's my story summarised, I hope I didn't bore you, I don't know why I even told you about myself as I have just only met you."
"Sorry to hear about your parents, it was an interesting story, sometimes we tend to misjudge a person without knowing their background," said Floop.
Sena sighed, both lay staring at the blank dark ceiling above them. They soon drifted off into dreamland.

III

Just as Sena had suggested both decided to spend the day planning for the dangerous journey into the forbidden land. Floop studied the map over and over. Sena prepared some *dried fly broth* which Floop gladly swooped up. Floop and Sena discussed each of the vital roles they would play. Floop reminded Sena of the big furry big toothed, pink tailed beast that Diggles had previously described. He also mentions that it would be best to move when the *Thumpers* moved. *Thumpers* moved around during the day so therefore they would only move during the day and rest under shelter during the night. The map was a great help to Floop as per his estimate it would take about two days to get to the green. Sena dared to ask Floop the question to which he really didn't have the answer.

"What do we do once we get to the green?" asked Sena.

Floop didn't have an answer, without questioning logic both him and Sena embarked on the adventure to seek out the green, but surely there was proof already that the green existed as per Diggles. Floop sat down and pondered on this for a while. Shaking his head in different directions supposedly having a conversation with himself in his mind.

"It does not look like we thought this one through did we, what if we don't make it?" said Sena.

Floop was still trying to make logic in his mind, then suddenly he stopped.

"Have you got some lead and paper?" requested Floop.

"Yes, I do."

"Well then, I suggest we never return!" said Floop.
"*What*!" Yelled Sena. "Have you lost your mind?"
"On the contrary, the idea is that for every two hours that we travel we place a flag with directions so that others may follow," suggested Floop.
"And would someone will follow it?"
"By now, Wisen and King Mosesha would have realized that we must be missing and would send a search party to rescue us," said Floop excitedly.
"That's a big chance we're taking," said Sena.
"Well it's a chance we going to have to take, they will find us, I hope!" said Floop.

Floop wrote on a piece of paper the following, '*Floop with Sena fellow Carpils', headed toward the Green, follow arrows.*" Neatly dated it and stuck it onto a stick and placed an arrow in the direction they were to proceed into- the *forbidden land*. Sena made the last arrangements before departure. Filled up tiny water canisters' from a water stream that leaked through the wall. Checked the small torches. Packed up and were now ready to venture into the forbidden lands.
Floop and Sena stood at the edge between the forbidden lands and the kingdom of the Carpils'. It was the furthest they have ever been to. Sena placed her hand into Floop's hand.
"Shall we," said Sena.

Both took their first step into the forbidden land. Immediately it felt as though they were transported into another world. Everything seemed different, darkness fell over the land, and there was a misty smog that surrounded them. The smell had changed to something they had never smelt before, it was very pungent. It was exactly as Diggles had described it before. Floop reminded Sena that they should always stay close to the wall and follow it to its end and never stray from each other.

"What if we lose each other?" asked Sena.

Floop had already memorised the map and handed it to Sena.

"Keep this with you, and if ever we get separated keep along the wall," suggested Floop.

They had already separated their hands as it was starting to get a bit uncomfortable. They took their first steps and immediately sunk into thick *moss* about knee high. It was thick, cold and moist. They struggled with the first few steps and after about an hour they were cleared off the moss and onto the ground. The ground beneath their feet was very slimy and sticky. They proceeded to the wall sat down to take some rest sitting against the dirt that laden the wall. Floop thought that it may be best to place another flag, he wrote, ***'Floop with Sena, alive, headed alongside the wall.'*** Dated it and placed another arrow in the direction they would travel. They didn't know the time as there was no sound of any *Thumpers* or any sound at all, it was just creepily silent. That scared Sena as she moved closer towards Floop and sat next to him. Floop didn't know whether to place his arm around Sena, so he did not. He just sat next to Sena uncomfortably. Remember Carpils' have good eyesight in the dark but were close sighted, so they were able to see far objects but it was very blurry. Both stared into the far darkness, they could make out figures moving in the thick moss but couldn't see clearly. Floop suggested they rest at this point until they hear the *Thumpers* from above. Sena drifted off into a sleep and fell onto Floop's lap. Floop decided to stay awake in the event of any danger he would be ready. He sat thinking to himself on ways to defend himself, especially Sena and soon realised that he had no official training in fighting. He imagined a few battle scenes in his mind, it's one thing to think about doing something and actually doing it with your body. Nonetheless, it kept him entertained, then the thought of fighting imaginary creatures. The land was very

silent except for a few ruffling noises that startled him. Floop continued with his splendid imagination and then imagination drifted into a fantastical dream. Floop was in the *3-G Race* amongst other young Carpils' ready and bound on their roaches.' Other village Carpils' were all in attendance watching the race with great eagerness. Floop waving at the crowd. King Mosesha seated within the crowd. The race started and Floop was racing hard against the young Carpils'. He was in fourth place slowly edging forwards into third than second. The crowd screaming his name. 'Floop, Floop' he was now riding faster getting closer to the leader with every stride that the roach made. He had finally overtaken the leader and he was in the first place just a little while longer to cross the finish line, the crowds now screaming his name. Floop turned his head to look at the crowds as he closed into to crossing the finish line, within the crowd, he could see Sena's face smiling and waving at him. The roach stumbled and Floop fell onto the ground! Floop awoke with a jerk, looked at Sena still sleeping on his lap and smiled to himself. He wondered why he had this feeling of warm and tingling sensations all over his body. He pondered on the thought that Sena may also feel the same way, but that quickly dissolved as Sena awoke.
"Sorry I might have dozed off," said an awakening Sena still yawning.
Floop stared at Sena in awe for a while, almost frozen stiff, and then realized he should answer back.
"All good," replied Floop nervously.

Floop needed to shake off this feeling quickly, in case
Sena suspected anything. He jumped up to his feet
promptly but lost his balance slightly then managed to
recoup himself.
"We need to make ground," said Floop.
Just then there was a ruffle that could be heard around
them, it made the hair on their skin from their neck,
down to their back and all the way to their fingers
stand on edge.
"Something is watching us," whispered Sena.
They both stood dead still not wanting to make any
sudden moves. The ruffling stopped.
"*It watches*," said Sena "we need to be careful from
now on."
Floop reminded Sena of what Diggles had told them
about placing faeces on himself to hide the smell.
Floop found some horrendous smelling faeces laying
on the floor close to them and suggested they rub it all
over themselves.
"Just in case," suggested Floop.
"No way am I rubbing that on me!" Sena yelled back.
"What other suggestions, do you have?" said Floop,
"We're like sitting flesh."
Sena pulled out the potion marked *'Flignog.'*
"Sprinkle some of this on us," suggested Sena, "It is
safer but makes us smell rather hideous."

Floop sprinkled some on himself and flinched with the terrible yucky smell. Sena smelt just as bad. The previous thoughts that Floop had of Sena suddenly disappeared. Both packed up their belongings. Floop checked that the flag was firmly in place. They patiently waited for the sound of the *Thumpers* above them. It wasn't too long when they heard the sound of *Thumpers*, dust fell from the carpet onto them. Sena sneezed and gave a giggle.

"We ought to get going now." Suggested Floop.

With each sound the *Thumpers* made, Sena and Floop moved along the wall. They had looked back and could see the far distance between themselves and the Carpil Kingdom. There was no turning back now, they continued walking, watching every step. It was a long journey. Floop stopped for a drink of water but had completely forgotten to offer Sena first. He promptly stopped drinking and offered Sena the flask, Sena accepted the gesture, drank, closed the tiny flask and placed it back in her satchel. They continued silently for some time until the *Thumpers* stopped. It was a very tiring trip on foot and wished they could have used the roaches'. They decided to rest and continue on the journey the next day. Floop decided to make another flag and placed it in the ground. Sena scouted the area for a place to sleep. The land was thick with smog and dust. Floop suggested that he prepares dinner showing off some of his skills to Sena. He made a *dried worm* stew. It didn't taste very good, but Sena politely ate it and applauded Floop on his cooking. Besides anything else other than *inside-out* worm soup. Floop felt flattered. Both sat down to enjoy the stew when they heard something approaching them. They froze. A ***big furry, pink tailed, toothed beast*** approached them sniffing. It started sniffing at Floop pressed against the wall. Floop hadn't been so scared in his life, he felt tears well up in his eyes, and knees go weak and stomach *twirling*. The furry beast smelt Floop from head to toe sniffing and snorting, Sena dropped the bowl of stew and the beast promptly turned and head directly for the fallen stew gobbling it up at once. The beast gave a last sniff and scurried away.

"Looks like the **Flignog** worked," whispered Sena in relief.

Floop didn't answer back immediately, merely because he couldn't get himself to talk. Tears flowed down his cheek and onto his lips. He shyly wiped them away.

"That was a close call," stuttered Floop.

"Hahahahah," laughed Sena.

"It's not funny, I almost messed my pants," retorted Floop.

Clearly, the braver between the two was Sena.

"We should take some rest, *baby boy*," teased Sena. Floop rather embarrassed promised himself that he would be much braver from now on. They both lay against the damp wall and drifted into sleep. Sena dreamed of the time she was six years and her parents were still alive.

They were abruptly awoken to find themselves facing many furry beasts about five in total sniffing them. They slowly stood up. The furry beast had returned with some friends this time and was very ravenous. Sena and Floop froze. One of the furry beasts smelt Sena and then moved over to smell Floop. *It stuck out its thin long tongue and licked Floop from belly to face. Snarled, expeditiously swooped Floop into its mouth whole.* The beast leisurely walked off with Floop in its mouth while the rest of the furry beasts continued sniffing at Sena….. Eventually, they turned lazily and walked away unsatisfied. Sena dropped to her knees. A cry of repudiation and horror burst from the lips of Sena. She sat in total shock. Floop was gone, she was on her own. Sena reeling from all the anger stood up and wiped her tears away. There was to time for crying.

Sena gathered her thoughts, pulled out the map that Floop had left with her. She was now determined more than ever to reach the green. With great bravery and without the sound of the *Thumpers* Sena fearlessly walked on across the land and deep into the moss, she strode relentlessly. Her feet started to ache but Sena continued on. Along the way she passed nasty floor creatures that crawled and snarled, none dared come close to her. They could probably smell the fearlessness that Sena now possessed. Eventually, Sena stopped at her own accord. She had completely forgotten to place a flag in the ground. Did it really matter she wondered to herself? Was this all really all worth it?

Coming to her senses, Sena wrote out on a piece of paper, ***'Sena alone, headed towards the green.'*** Stuck the paper onto a stick and with virtuosity stuck the flag into the ground. She walked along the wall, recalling the time she had spent with Floop. Tears rolled down her face. An intense feeling of loneliness crept into her soul. She missed Floop.

Sena found the courage to stand up and continued walking.

No one could have been more surprised. Sena stared at the presence, unthinkable, unbelievable. There were no words to describe the unthinkable truth. There, before her eyes stood the leaves of the ***'GREEN'*** just as Diggles had described. Overcome with sheer delight. Sena jumped without hesitation into the thick moist luscious leaves. She made it!

Sena tossed and turned amongst the leaves. Time felt limitless. Still, in sheer admiration, Sena stepped back to view the beauty of the leaves. She thought to herself, Floop would have been ecstatic. Hastily, she tried to find the source. Where it was coming from? All that could be observed was a crack in the wall and the leaves had grown through them. She tried knocking against the wall, nothing! She tried knocking harder it would not move or even crack. Abruptly, there was a loud **Thud**! And another **Thud!** The furry beast was banging its head repeatedly against the wall. **Thud!** It was going crazy, back and forth banging against the wall. There was something satisfying in watching the furry beast banging its head. A delightful sound was heard, the sound that can only be described as rewarding. A chunk of the wall fell in, the brightest light shone through into Sena's eyes. A view that had never been seen before slowly emerged through the hole, she could see the vast green in all its glory. *Marvellous* and beautiful beyond any comprehension.

The furry beast ran away cowardly, Sena felt a nudge on her shoulder and brushed it away. She was, of course, looking at the *Promised Land*. She felt another nudge, somewhat annoyed, she turned around. Standing right in front of her, it was Floop! Sena stood in *wonderment* staring blankly at Floop. Was she dead, was this the afterlife? It did not matter to her. Sena hugged Floop with all her might.
"You idiot!" Sena yelled.
Floop laughing, "Thought I was a goner didn't you."
"How did you…?"
"You underestimate me, if I could tame one hundred roaches', what is a furry beast to me," bragged Floop.

They both embraced each other again. They both
stared at the green through the hole in the wall. It was
well worth the journey.
"Looks like we made it!" said Floop.
Both could not take their eyes off of the view, a
gratifying view it was.

Wisen was right! Their perseverance had paid off.
Floop and Sena closed their eyes and together stepped
onto the green. Their bare feet felt the warmth of the
green welcoming them. Opening their eyes, there was
lush green, beautiful flowers, sweet-smelling nectar
surrounding them. They ran like two *whippersnappers*
into the green. Running and jumping. Sena spotted a
stream of water and jumped in, Floop instinctively
followed her. Though both did not know how to swim.
It was shallow enough. Sploshing and splashing water
on each other. Jubilation and euphoria filled the air.
Both now lay on the banks of the stream, looking up
into the sky, there was no roof, no darkness, just clear
dazzling sky. Floop took a deep breath of clean air that
filled his tiny lungs.
"Smashing isn't it?" Floop making the rhetorical
statement as though it should come as a stunning
surprise.
"Simply delightful," responded Sena.
Drenched in lethargy, they both lay staring into the
sky. Sena began to sing,
**"For there's a song you sang to me and there was a
fire of light**
**The flame in me grew so bright it lightened the entire
night**
**We live we laugh we sing tonight, oh what a
beautiful sight**

For the flame that lit the night was indeed filled with purity and light
So we'll live and laugh and sing our lives in just one night"
Floop listened in such delight.
Sena and Floop decided it best to explore the green further. But where to start? Sena reminded Floop of the Ye ol' book contents and suggested they promptly start searching for other Carpils', Floop corrected her as he stated that they were now Groundies.

IIII

In the intervening time, back at the Carpil Palace, Wisen was pacing up and down in the palace hall room. King Mosesha sat quietly at the end of the long table. Kitchen staff brought out a meal with a few drinks and quickly exited feeling the tension. Diggles had decided to tuck into the meal, King Mosesha had no appetite. There was an awkward silence that filled the room. Wisen deep in thought.

"Whatever do we do?" asked the King, breaking the silence.

Wisen stopped pacing and decided to sit down at the table, had himself a drink and folded his arms.

"Seems like we have no other choice," answered Wisen.

Diggles continued eating and crunching at the pieces of *fried worm*.

"Can you stop that annoying crunching!" yelled Wisen, "we have a serious situation on our hands."

Diggles pushed his plate away in annoyance, he looked at Wisen dumbfound.

"What would you expect me to do, I am merely an explorer," said Diggles.

Wisen stared at Diggles with his bulging eye and answered, "You may be just an explorer, but you possess great knowledge that will be used, can you still remember the map to the green?"

"Of course I can," answered Diggles confidently.

"Then may you be as kind as to draw as many maps as you can," instructed Wisen.

Diggles left the hall room to fetch lead and paper. Wisen turned his attention to the King still sitting in deep thought. Wisen pulled his chair closer to the King.

"The situation as it stands dear King, is that Floop and Sena have travelled alone to find the green,' said Wisen, "We don't know what dangers may have befallen them and if they are still alive."

*"Hope, Wisen, **hope**!"* responded the King.

"Don't be foolish, two young Carpils', what are the odds," retorted Wisen, "We must send reinforcements."

"Who do we send? Most if not all Carpils' are ill-equipped for this sort of task, we don't have any warriors," said the King.

"Everyone is a warrior in their own right, given the right situation!" exclaimed Wisen.

"We do have excellent food hunters, some good on the bow and others on the sword," suggested the King. Wisen agreed! King Mosesha summoned Uni the palace guard and instructed him to venture into the village and return with the village hunters by order of the King -strictly, confidential and urgent. Uni confused accepted the instruction and proceeded into the village in search of the hunters.

The Carpil village outside the gates of the palace stretched some distance. The village widely spaced out with Carpils' living outside the village and some within the village city main trade market. Many Carpils' filled the village from one to two hundred and eleven years of age. Streets were sandy with shops lining adjacent to them. From butchers, blacksmiths, bakers, tailors to even a funeral parlour. It was like any city except it was built from scraps that had fallen through the carpet. Mostly the construction was made out of wooden boxes and neatly painted with different colours of nail polish. There were a mail room, a bar and even a play theatre. Roaches' used as transport filled the streets. The economy was run on trade items, therefore all of the Carpils' had work. They either traded their skills or bargained with items. There was no exchange of money. The same principle applied to them when they were still known as Groundies. Uni walked through the dusty streets knocking on shop doors and at villager's homes. Often sticking up signs at shop fronts and light poles strewn with old Christmas lighting. Whispers began within the village Carpils'. Something was going on. Uni continued on his tiresome mission and felt parched. He decided to stop at *'Jiggle bar'* for a beaker of *stink-beetle* ale and to his surprise, all four of the village hunters, Stix, Stones, Rok and Hardes were seated drinking ale and teasing young Carpil ladies. Uni decided to order his *stink-beetle* ale first and slugged it down, wiping the remaining froth from his beard, he pulled his helmet straight and walked over to these seated hunters.
"Oy, you bunch, the King requires your presence at once!" yelled Uni.

"On what business, can't you see we're busy," yelled Rok back.

"It is important secret business it is," retorted Uni. Stix still teasing the Carpil ladies stood up and tried questioning Uni further.

"Well then, by order of the King I suggest we make haste to the palace," said Stones.

They all left *'Jiggles bar'* walking through the city streets, Carpils' stopped what they were doing and all well most of them stopped and stared at the men as they trudged towards the palace gates.

There was a sombre atmosphere in the palace as the huntsmen entered the hall-room. Stix and Stones identical brothers, the only difference being one had white hair and the other black hair but both had no beards. They had their bows strapped around their shoulders. Dressed in brown pants and woollen vests. Slightly leaner and taller than Rok and Hardes. Rok was shorter and fatter than the rest of them with a long brown beard. Dressed in a long black and brown jacket that touched his feet. Hardes was largely built and muscular. Dressed in a heavy jacket resembling the fur of a furry beast. Rok and Hardes both kept their swords dangling from their waist. Wisen and the King still immersed in deep conversation as Hardes the bigger built from the huntsmen, in a deep voice, interrupted the discussion taking place between Wisen and the King.

"You have summoned us King Mosesha," said a bowing Hardes.

Wisen and the King turned to the four huntsmen.

"*Ahhh,* welcome, we have been expecting you, please sit," suggested the King.

The King called in the usher to arrange drinks for the party of guests.

"Huntsman, not warriors, but warriors you shall be!" said Wisen.

Stix, Stones, Rok and Hardes sat with muddled looks on their faces. Wisen stood up and walked to the far end of the table, taking on the daunting task of having to explain the story of Diggles from the forbidden lands to proof of the green. Wisen went on further to explain how the courageous Floop and Sena ventured on their own to find the green. Rok stroked his long beard. Diggles entered the hall-room holding several drawings of the map. Diggles continued to the fill in the gaps of the forbidden forest and intensely explained the furry beasts. A loud robust discourse ensued for several minutes.

"So what is expected from us?" yelled Stix.

"It was not what is expected from you it is what is required from all of you," said Wisen. We need the four of you brave Carpils' to venture into the forbidden lands, find Floop and Sena and return them back safely."

"What about the green?" asked Rok.

"The green, the green?" Shout King Mosesha.

The green was the ultimate allotment. All the Carpils' would be eager to return to the green. Discussions followed with great debate.

"It is decided then," yelled Hardes, "we the four of us shall venture into the forbidden land, rescue the two delinquent Carpils' and seek out the green."

Stix, Stones, Rok and Hardes agreed. Diggles handed out copies of the map to each of them and carefully explained the pathway and dangers that may befall them. King Mosesha summoned for the blacksmith and instructed him to sharpen the swords and supply sufficient arrows.

"We shall leave at the break of dawn tomorrow, said Stones.

Wisen and King Mosesha bid the newly acclaimed warriors on their way. Up to now, whispers had grown within the Carpil village. There was a sense of intrigue and wonderment. Wisen looked out of the palace walls into the Carpil village. Carpils' were gathering around shops and shared hearsay *chitchat*. At this time, in barged Petunia in manic.

"What's this I hear about the green?" demanded Petunia.

Wisen calmed Petunia, sat her down and explained the discovery of the green and the daring attempt from Floop and Sena.

"You see I am not *bonkers*!" exclaimed Petunia, "but what's to become of Sena, my granddaughter."

Again Wisen rationally explained to Petunia that Stix, Stones, Rok and Hardes were sent to rescue Sena. The king sat quietly deep in thought, possibly wondering about his dear Queen and Princess.

"We should tell the villagers, we owe it to them," suggested Petunia.

Wisen pondered on the idea.

"Maybe we should, what say you King?" asked Wisen. The King answered, "Maybe we should, the Carpils' been looking for **hope** all the long years, maybe we should."

The following day, King Mosesha called for a village meeting with the Carpils' from all the villagers across the kingdom from the youngest to the oldest, all were expected to attend. There was a buzz amongst the Carpils' as they all gathered in front of the palace gates, hundreds of Carpils' filled the village. There was a sense of unease amongst everyone. Anxious talking took place amongst the Carpils' as the last time King Mosesha addressed everyone so formally was fifty-two years ago when all of the dreaded carpet was laid across them all.

"Where's the king?" yelled one of the villagers. The rest of the Carpils' followed shouting repeatedly, "where's the king?"

By now Stix, Stones, Rok and Hardes would be approaching the forbidden land. King Mosesha climbed up the wooden stairs assisted by his needle walking stick into a high podium outside the palace gates. The crowd went silent.

King Mosesha addressed the crowd, ***My fellow Carpils', today I do not stand in front of you as your King, but as a fellow Carpil just as yourselves, we all have been through a lot over the last fifty-two years, but with resilience and perseverance we have managed to build ourselves a new home. We should be proud of ourselves, your persistence paved the way to harmony within grief. We have lost many of our friends and family during the time before we called ourselves Carpils'. The rumours that you have heard are true! The green has been found!"***

Most of the older Carpils' gasped in excitement, "*the Green has been found!*"

The younger Carpils' unaware of the existence of the green was given a quick summary.

"Hope!" yelled the King, ***"hope is what we all hung onto and today I am glad to say, there is still hope!"*** The Carpils' all cheered.

King Mosesha continued, ***"We have sent our huntsmen out through the forbidden lands, the time has come to follow them to our land, the green!"***

"When do we leave," yelled a villager.

"Collect all that you can carry, for tomorrow we reclaim what was once ours!" yelled the King.

Wisen in haste, grabbed Diggles that stood unaware.

"Where are we off to in such a rush?" questioned Diggles.

"I have forgotten something very important and I need your help" responded Wisen

Wisen and Diggles mounted two Roaches'. The heavyweight on the roaches' could be heard as a small a squeal was heard. Wisen and Diggles made their way to Wisen's home. Upon reaching, Wisen quickly dismounted his roach proceeded to his front door and swung it upon. Diggles followed. Wisen searched frantically around his house, throwing books on the floor, searching behind potion shelves. He was in a panic, searching. At this time the whole house was turned upside down. Wisen through the scattered mess on the floor continued searching.

"I must find it!" yelled Wisen.

Diggles also joining in the search.

"What are we looking for?" asked Diggles.

Wisen ignored Diggles and searched high and low, in every crevice. *Eventually, he stopped, he had found what he had been searching for, and he quickly wrapped an old cloth around it and placed it within his sack.*

"We need to leave at once," said Wisen.

Diggles still very confused, agreed. Wisen requested a copy of the map from Diggles and studied it carefully. "We shall have to proceed adjacent to the wall, we need to make haste," announced Wisen.
Wisen and Diggles didn't waste much time, they promptly mounted the roaches' and off they sped towards the forbidden land. They had soon arrived at the rubbish pile that Floop and Sena had previously passed. The old Carpil man busy scuffing through the piles of wanted items as usual.
"Slew!" yelled Wisen.
Wisen had known the old Carpil man from the time before.
"Wisen, what might you be doing here?" Slew asked.
"Haven't got the time for chitchat Slew," answered Wisen. "Have you had any young-in Carpil pass this way?"
"I bloody well did, they poisoned me they did, if I get my hands on them!" yelled Slew.
"You would be doing no such thing," warned Wisen, "which direction did they go?"
"Don't know, they just took some items, have no idea where they went," replied Slew.
"You of no use to us!" yelled Wisen, "good day to you."
Wisen and Diggles proceeded on towards the forbidden land. At the edge still stood Floop and Sena's Flag they had left. Just below the sign scribbled in the words 'Stix, Stones, Rok, and Hardes all four, not less headed in this direction.'
Wisen had decided earlier not to follow the wall and enter directly into the deep of the forbidden forest. That way they could still ride on the roaches' and hopefully create a diversion for the Huntsman.

V

Floop and Sena looked at the far outstretched land in wonderment. The **"GREEN'** endless. Floop turned around to look at the huge building that stood erect above the carpet. It was painted a beautiful pasty white. Big large windows and shades adorned the building. Buildings set next to each other in splendour. A *Thumper* stood at the door, fair-skinned, with long black hair, wearing a very colourful paisley skirt that hung from shoulder to foot. There was some material bound around the feet. How funny looking Floop thought to himself. Sena giggled to herself. The *Thumpers* were not their concern, for now, they were interested in finding the Groundies. The open land stretched so far that Sena and Floop could not decide on the direction that they would take. During this time, Floop totally forgot to place any flag in the ground. They walked heedfully across the land passing big trees, small, tiny trees, all types of trees in all shapes and sizes. They stopped to smell the sweet flowers, often tasting a few as this was a foreign land to them. They discovered huge bright red voluptuous strawberries growing from just above the ground. Sena immediately took a hefty bite into one of the strawberries. The taste tickled her whole mouth as she crunched down into it, sweet juices flowed within her mouth touching every taste bud. Her fingers, toes cheeks felt warm at the same. She swayed back at forth as the sweet, plush juices dripped down her throat. Floop at Sena as though she was going *whoopsy*.

He took a bite into the strawberry, it didn't have the same reaction it had with Sena. *Ah well!* He thought to himself and left Sena to continue swaying back in forth in a dream-like state whilst he continued eating the strawberry, it did taste fairly good. Some time passed when Sena came back to her senses. Both decided to continue their exploration they passed oddly shaped grotesque mounds that protruded from the ground up. There were many of these mounds in different shapes and heights some as high as seventeen feet, many holes were on the surface of the mounds. Much was not thought of these mounds as they passed them merrily. There was still no sign of any Groundies, all of a sudden Floop out the corner of his eye caught a glimpse of a few which he thought were Groundies, quickly scurrying into holes of one the mounds. Floop ran screaming and shouting with all his might towards the mound. Just as quickly as he saw them just as quick they had vanished into the mound. Sena had now caught up to Floop and both examined this mysterious mound.

"Where did they go!" yelled Floop, "I saw them."

"Are you sure?" replied Sena.

"Yes, I am sure," retorted Floop.

This was unusual, though their whole surroundings were strange, the mounds stood out as the creepiest. It sends shivers down their spines. Floop peering down one of the holes almost fell in, Sena grabbed him and pulled him into safety.

"Are you daft?" asked Sena, "we can't be certain if they were even Groundies, plus you have no idea where these holes lead to."

Floop agreed, however, they thought if Groundies were at this mound surely they should stay awhile in the event they do return. It was decided to rest for the night near the mound. As the sun dipped and the moon began to shine brightly above them, both Sena and Floop lay awake just looking at the beautifully-woven carpet of the sky above them. Filled with otherworldly sparkling lights.

Break of day shone across the land as Sena and Floop opened their eyes to a new day, a new beginning. Floop decided to take a leisure walk to a stream for a drink of fresh water when suddenly he stopped and slowly carried himself to Sena. Nudging Sena.
"What do you want?' yelled Sena.
"Shoosh!" whispered Floop, "look over there."
They both knelt down between the leaves of the grass. At the base of the mound, they could see Groundies, dressed in old torn rags, dirty with unkempt hair and beards. Thin as sticks they were, no traditional big bellies like the Carpils…. Dragging heaving pieces of mud and stone. Sena was about to lunge out towards them, Floop pulled her down.
"Look over there," whispered Floop.

Sena strained her eyes, there stood many creatures that resembled roaches except they stoop upright, about an inch and a half tall, dark brown in colour, wearing black leathery amour. Their legs awkwardly bent inward, stood firmly on the ground supported by pincers as toes. Faces looked like the roaches except much pronounced and harder. Two sharp circular incisor teeth protruded through their mouths. Four hands in total, spears in hand, and little antenna's that stuck out their heads. Though not clear, it would be assumed that they were shouting orders at the Groundies to keep working. Floop and Sena watched in repugnance.

"Ay, what are you doing here?" came a shout from behind.

Floop and Sena turned steadily stoop up before them both stood a creature similar to the ones the ordering the Groundies around except he had a long deep scratch across his left cheek.

"What are you doing here?" yelled the creature, "wait, you don't look like them sorts, who are you?"

Sena decided to answer back, "We're just travellers if you allow we would be making our way."

"No!" said the creature shaking his head, "you aren't travellers, I can smell it." The creature gestured towards them and took a huge sniff.

"We are travellers," answered Floop, stepping backwards.

"You two aren't going nowhere, you coming with me, let's see what King Iso makes of you," said the creature.

The creature shoved and poked at Floop and Sena.

"Be careful!" yelled Floop.

The creature ignored Floop's' request, shoved them into a hole at a nearby mound that went deeper into the ground... It was dark, gloomy and cold. The good florescent eyesight assisted Floop and Sena greatly as they made their way through underneath mudded up walls. They approached a round circular hall that had many tunnels surrounding it. They could see Groundies thumping at the wall with picks as they were shoved into a long deep tunnel. The narrow tunnel seemed to stretch far. They were uncomfortable being poked behind by the creature with his spear to keep moving.

"Almost there now, the King will be delighted," he said squeamishly.
They approached the end of the tunnel, into a larger round circular mound, small holes made through the mound lit up the place. There were other creatures standing as guards at the mouth to another entrance, wearing shiny silver spiked shoulder waddings and helmets
"Search these two," ordered the creature.
Guard creatures surrounded Floop and Sena and awkwardly searched them, rigidly pulling off their back straps and other devices. The guard pulled the drawn-out map from beneath Floop's' vest and handed it to scratched face creature.

Once thoroughly searched. They entered another circular mound, much bigger, it lay above the ground, well lit up from bigger holes from the top of the mound. The round walls were all made from dried hard mud, surrounding the walls were mud tables with various metal objects and bowls on them. There were mud chairs surrounding a gigantic mud chair. On it sat another creature.

"Who dares disturb me on this wonderful day?" yelled the seated creature.

"It is I Naut dear King Iso, look at what I have found wondering your kingdom," said Naut pushing Floop and Sena towards the seated King Iso.

King Iso stood up much larger than the other creatures, about two inches tall, more pronounced features. Dressed in a long black woolly robe with white edges that slang down to his feet. Majestic looking, wearing a silver pointy crown. King Iso walked closer to Floop and Sena examining them carefully. The King stood gigantically over them, Naut cautiously handed him the drawn-out map. King Iso smiled and rubbed his hands together.

"Where are my manners,' said King Iso, "please sit." Floop and Sena uncomfortably sat in the mud chairs provided to them, Naut and King Iso remained standing.

"Let me introduce myself, I am ***King Iso, the King of Kings,*** King of all the land," said the King boastfully. Pointing to Naut, "And this is my most loyal and champion rider Naut, and what might be your names?" Floop answered nervously, "*Uhhh…*they call me Floop and this is Sena, we're just travellers as we stated before."

"Travellers you say, I know your type," said King Iso.

"Yes, travellers, we mean no harm, just passing
through, if you would be so kind we will be on our
way," responded Sena.

King Iso took some time examining the map that Naut
had handed to him. Looked at Sena and Floop with
'not born yesterday stare' and continued to study the
map. The king sat down on his chair directly in front
of Sena and Floop.

"I never thought I would ever see the likes of you,"
said the King sarcastically. "I never thought any of
you Groundies made it."

"We're Carpils," retorted Sena.

"Feisty one aren't you?" said King Iso. "Well then let
me tell you how you came to be. It was fifty-two years
ago, I was just forty at the time. Us **'ANARTS'**, that is
the name we go by, we only live to a maximum of fifty
years and here I stand ninety-two years old, you know
why? Let me answer that question, you ***'Groundies'***
are marvellous folk, after discovering the secret potion
of the Groundies, age became limitless, however,
unlike Groundies we need to constantly take a potion
that is made by only Groundies, a *long-life potion.*
Therefore, it was only obvious that I would make all
the Groundies my slaves" laughed the King.

"That's horrible!" yelled Sena.

King Iso continued, "From the tip of your nose to as far as you can see, I rule. I am the King. It was not so easy, we hitched a ride with the man that came. Foreign land to us, surrounded by *yucky*, little Groundies. As I mentioned before, I was forty years of age reaching old age. I managed to befriend one of the Kings of the Groundies, there were many kingdoms that surrounded these lands. I offered my aid in services to the Groundies King and in return, he promised me the *secret potion* in my services as his forager. I assembled my strongest soldiers and humbly served the Groundies King. Fifteen years had passed. We **'ANARTS'** were now able and strong with long life. It was then that I decided to hatch my plan. There was a lost Princess within the midst of the kingdom, named Shamora, I had plans for her. When we weren't foraging, we dug tunnels in the ground clearly out of sight of the King and any Groundies. It was on a hot, humid day, the Groundies King invited me over for a sumptuous feast as one of the Groundies had reached two hundred and twelve years to celebrate his farewell…. All the Groundies would be in attendance including Princess Shamora. It was the perfect day, I rallied all my soldier Anarts, whilst the feast continued in a jovial manner with all the Groundies seated along a lengthy table. Princess Shamora sat at the end of the table, quick as light, Naut snatched her away from the table, covered her mouth and bound her hands and disappeared with her into the tunnels. Nobody had noticed the Princess had gone missing. We all continued with the feast, I bid the King and the rest of the Groundies farewell and made my way deep to into the tunnels. There I met the beautiful Princess Shamora. ***What is a King without a Queen?*** I quickly arranged a marriage between us and I was a newly crowned King. Of course, genetically we could never conceive any children so I married another Anart as my second wife to grow my colony. ***Princess Shamora*** would now be the Queen of the Groundies and me the handsome King. Queen Shamora is kept in one of the mounds, hidden from all as my prisoner. The next day I sent Naut to deliver the news to the Groundies King that I am the new King with Princess Shamora as my keep. There was resistance from the Groundies King as he struck Naut across his face, leaving that terrible scar across his cheek. The Groundies across the lands rebelled against us, but of course, they were far too weak for my strong soldiers, we captured most of the Groundies and killed the rest. Pestilent *buggers* they were. We started rebuilding using the Groundies for slaves. Mounds and mounds were built each one bigger than the other. I had made a deal with Queen Shamora if she continued to make me the long-life potion I would spare the rest of the Groundies. Now I see you two, you mentioned, your names were Floop and Sena. Well I thought I am the King of all the lands, looks like some of you have survived and stayed in hiding, I am the only King!"

"You're no King, you're a murderer!" yelled Sena. King Iso walked up to Sena looked deeply into her eyes.

"If it's only the two of you, it looks like I may need a third wife," said King Iso.

"Never!" yelled Floop.

"Naut, take them away, put him in the dungeon and take feisty one to the towers," instructed King Iso.

Naut instructed the guards to take Sena up to the
towers. Floop fiercely trying to resist. Naut hit Floop
over the head and proceeded to drag him through the
cold dusty tunnels. They were soon at a mud dungeon,
surrounded by torture devices and cells filled with
Groundies crying and pleading for mercy. Naut threw
Floop into a Dungeon and slammed the gate shut. The
mud cell was occupied by another Groundie, laying
quietly on a mud bed. Floop tried in vain to pry open
the gate, it was locked tight. Anart guards lined the
dungeon chambers, often shouting vile offensive
language at the Groundies in the cells.
"It's no use," came a voice within the mud cell.
"They can't do this to us," yelled Floop.
The seated Groundie sat upon the mud bed. He has
much muscular built than the rest of the thin
Groundies. Long black hair and a short beard. Wearing
leather stringed vest and pants. Many scars adorned his
body, he spoke in a deep voice.
"Not much we can do, it's the only type of life we
have," said the Groundie.
"There must be some kind of mistake," responded
Floop sitting on the mud bed opposite the Groundie.
"Name's Groop,' said the Groundie.
Floop in a nonchalant response, "they call me Floop,
what's the story with this place?"

Groop answered, "this place is all we know, well there was a time many years ago when we roamed freely, that was thirty-seven years ago when we were all enslaved to Iso, he calls himself King. He is no King of ours. All the kingdoms were taken by him one by one. Female Groundies were taken as servants, children and males were taken as slaves to build tunnels and mounds, you look like a Groundie but not so weak. I don't know how you survived so long without being captured?"

Floop felt comfortable with Groop and decided to explain to him that he was indeed a Groundie, however aptly called Carpils. He went on to explain how they had survived living under the carpet, King Mosesha and the rest of the Carpil kingdom. Floop also went to explain the relation between King Mosesha and Princess Shamora.

"Bly me," responded Groop, "I would never have thought there were other Groundies."

"Well seems like I am in a fine mess now," replied Floop.

An Anart guard shoved mud bowls filled with food through the cells.

"Enjoy my lovelies," said the Guard.

Floop examined the mud bowls filled with a brown thick, sticky, most horrible smelling blob of food he had ever seen.

"That's the meal of the day, Anarts eat mostly wood, and this my friend is the leftovers," said Groop, "you might as well get used to it, you're going to be here a long time."

Floop refused the blob of food and briskly pushed it away holding his nose in disgust. He lay on the hard surface of the mud bed. Groop ate the sticky blob with his fingers, swallowing each blob whole with each mouthful.

"Day after tomorrow is the **Big Race**," said Groop between mouthfuls.

"What race?" asked Floop intrigued, sitting up.

"Every month, there is a spectacular race, King Iso and most of the Anarts attend. I am one of the riders, that's why I am not used as one of the slaves. I am part of the entertainment," said Groop.

"What do you race?" asked Floop, "please tell me more."

"There are twelve racers in all, most of them the best of Anarts, six of us Groundies race with them, and we race on **Ratz**," said Groop.

Floop asked in intrigue, "Has any Groundie won the race?"

"Once only once, the winner killed in front of the cheering Anarts, dishonourable and disgusting it was," replied Groot, "we never dare win!"

"Do you think I would be able to race?' asked Floop.

"Don't know are you any good?" asked Groop.

"I think so," replied Floop.

"Well then, I shall suggest to the guards that you race," said Groot, "better get some rest, guards don't like it when we *chitchat* too long."

They both lay onto the cold mud beds, Floop had a daring yet conniving plan.

Sena was taken to a large secure mound and flung into it. The inside of the mound was well decorated with flowers and little pretty objects. There wasn't any mud chairs like the rest of the mounds. It had nicely carved chairs with a large bed dressed with silky blankets. On the bed sat a startled Princess, well now Queen Shamora. She was dressed in a silky white long dress with silver shiny silver lining around it. Long beautiful black hair that curled at the edges. Given that she hardly looked a day older than thirty even though she was seventy-two years old. Her skin shone brightly as the light touched it. Sena tried to open the gates that had been tightly locked behind her.

"Who might you be?" asked Princess Shamora.

"Never mind whom I might be, how do I get out of here!" yelled Sena."

"I have tried many a time, but failed," replied Queen Shamora.

"You might be the Queen Shamora," said Sena sarcastically.

Queen Shamora responded politely, "I am no Queen, you can call me Shamora, and what might be your name?"

"Apologies, for being so rude, it's just that I should not be here," answered Sena, "my name is Sena from the kingdom of Carpils."

"Carpils?" asked Princess Shamora.

"Yip, from below the carpet, I am guessing you're lost Princess Shamora," answered Sena sitting on one of the chairs, "Looks like you have a nice place here while the rest of the Groundies live as slaves."

Princess Shamora was very intrigued with the Carpils and how Sena would have known about her.

"I do not care for this around me, King Iso provides all of this stuff in an attempt to appease me," said Princess Shamora, "I am a prisoner like the rest of the Groundies, bowing her head. "May I ask you a question?"
"Sure why not, it does not look like I am going anywhere soon" replied Sena.
"How do you know that I am a lost Princess?" asked Princess Shamora.
Sena gave Princess Shamora a detailed account of the Carpils, how fifty two years ago as Wisen described the story, the land was covered with carpet and of how she and Floop had decided to seek out the *'GREEN'* and find the rest of Carpils. Sena described her repulse upon seeing that state the Groundies were in. Sena continued with her verbal diarrhoea…
"Sorry to interrupt you, but I thought I heard you mention King Mosesha." said Princess Shamora, "is he still alive?"
Sena scratching her head answered, "ah yes, completely forgot, yes, he is still alive, lives a lonely life within the palace walls."
"Thank goodness," said a relieved Princess Shamora.
"Whatever became of Queen Pearl?" asked Sena.

"Princess Shamora replied, "If my memory serves me correct, about fifty-two years ago, when *man* came and disrupted the peace in our lands, erected big buildings. It was on one frightful day we were all displaced, I remember Groundies running and screaming. We lost many that day including my father King Mosesha. My mother queen Pearl was not saved, within the chaos, sadly my mother lost her life. With our dear King and Queen lost, the rest of us Groundies were absorbed into a nearby Kingdom. Slowly we rebuilt. We left *man* alone and they left us alone. The cunning Anart Iso befriended the Groundie King, with the assistance of the Anarts the future looked brighter. It all ended with King Iso's greed for power. I was taken and forced to marry Iso, making him the automatic King, King Iso. I am always required to look my best in front of the Groundies and Anarts as their Queen. I still hold onto my father, King Mosesha's words. *'Hope' always have hope,'* it may seem that *hope* has arrived in the shape of you."

"You don't understand," said Sena, "King Iso wants to marry me, make me his third wife!"

"Cheeky, greedy bugger, chances are we will want to probably marry you on the day of the big races," said Princess Shamora, "which is the day after tomorrow."

King Iso summoned Naut to his royal conference hall to discuss a few matters. Naut entered the hall in his usual demeanour. King Iso stood alongside a long table, many pieces of paper with writing and drawings on them scattered across the table. On the table sat a massive wooden board upon it stood wooden characters in different colours. King Iso called it his strategy board. It had assisted the King many a time conquering the various Groundie kingdoms. Naut walked up to the table. It was just Naut and King Iso present in the room, usually, the place would have not less than twenty of the Anart generals. King Iso explained to Naut that this is a private meeting between the two of them. King Iso deep in thought, staring at the different pages that lay across the table. Walked around the table to view each paper. The papers contained ideas that the King had planned. Naut looking confused stood still whilst the King circled the table often rubbing his chin and mumbling to himself.
"Naut," said King Iso sternly.
"Yes, King Iso, how may I be of service?" asked Naut.

King Iso stating, "I am the King of all Kings, there can never be any other King besides me, now with these two young Groundies appearing, it gives hope to the rest of the Groundies. ***Hope does not exist***. I need to ensure that marrying the young Groundie, Sela, Senee or something like that, I would ensure loyalty from the Groundies and enforce my virility among the Anarts. I cannot be portrayed as weak I am not. I have decided to marry that girl on the day of *'Big Race'* in front of everyone. I think this time around instead of just the Anarts I would expect all the Groundies to attend. They should know who is in charge. I am the King. I am in a precarious situation as I do not know where or if there are any other Groundies around. I would need to obtain as much information as possible. Naut I would expect you to use your charm to extract as much information from the girl, do you understand?'

"Yes King Iso," answered Naut, "But what will happen to the girl after the marriage."

"I do not really care what becomes of her, place her in one of the mounds and let her rot, I suppose, I really don't have any need for her," said King Iso.

"I shall do as you wish," responded Naut, "there is something else I would like to discuss with you."

"Out with it then!" yelled King Iso.

"Well, the young Carpil boy Floop has requested to ride in the **'Big Race'**, and I was thinking it would be a good idea, I would easily beat him in the race, that I am certain of. It would also boost your status, adding further insult to the Groundies."

"I have an idea!" said King Iso, "That young Groundie boy, why don't you suggest that he rides the race, what do you think of my idea Naut."

"Great idea King Iso, I would never have thought about it myself,' said Naut.

"I need you to prepare the grounds for the race," said King Iso, "make sure all the Ratz are well fed, invite all the Anarts and demand every single Groundie attend. I wish to have a huge podium erected at the finish line. I am expecting you to win the race Naut. Take every measure to win, I want to embarrass the Groundies. It's going to be a wonderful day!"

"Should I make arrangements for the second Anart Queen to attend?" suggested Naut.

"That fat hag, all she is good for, is bearing offspring, leave her be!" retorted King Iso.

Both discussed further plans on the seating arrangements. Anarts on one side and the Groundies at the far end though in full view of the wedding that would take place. King Iso instructed Naut proper sizing of clothing for Sena, suggesting she should look majestic. The arrangements should also be made with the high Anart cleric to conduct the wedding. Naut exited the hall and promptly headed to Floop.

King Iso sat on his mud throne and stated loudly; ***"I am the King, the King of all Kings!"***

Naut proceeded through the long, winding tunnels to the mud dungeon. He walked pass Groundies tied to walls. The place stank of faeces. Naut looked into various mud cells looking for the cell that kept Floop. He called an Anart guard to assist in the search, there were too many cells and he had forgotten which cell he had flung Floop into. The guard pointed the mud cell Floop and Groop were securely held in. Naut walked towards the cell and banged on the steel. It made a huge ring that startled Floop and Groop who were deep in conversation.

"Ay you-you, the young one!" yelled Naut.

Floop approached the gate, much calmer than he was when he was first flung into the cell.

"You again!" said Floop

"I have come on the King's request", replied Naut.

"What does your so-called King, want from me?" questioned Floop.

"Have respect, he is your new King," insisted Naut.

"So what does your King want?" requested Floop.

"He has accepted you as a rider for the ***'Big Race'*** all the Anarts and Groundies will be present. The King wanted me to personally give you the rules," said Naut slyly.

"What if don't want to race?"

"You don't have a choice, race or join the rest as slaves," professed Naut.

"There is no lesser of both evils," retorted Floop, "but so be it, if your King so wishes, I shall."

"Not so hasty," said Naut, "there are rules."

"Which are?"

"You will race with Groop and four other Groundies, there are just two rules, remember them carefully, rule one, you shall bow to the King."

Floop responded sarcastically, "and the second rule?"
"Rule two, and remember it carefully," warned Naut,
"Rule two is that you will never win, do you
understand?"
"You saying if I understand this correctly, we're
allowed to race and not win, what happens if I win?"
asked Floop.
"There can be only one winner and that winner is me if
you so wish to win the race, try by all means but
remember to your own peril," answered Naut.
Naut banged hard against the cell gates, Floop did not
even flinch.
"You have been warned!" stated Naut and proceeding
to leave the smelly dungeon.
Floop turned to Groot with head cupped between his
hands.
"Did I not tell you," said Groop.
"I am going to win the race," said Floop.
"How so?" asked Groop.
"I have a plan, Naut mentioned that all the Anarts and
Groundies will be present," said Floop, "Groop you're
going to play a vital role."
"No, no, no, I am not part of any plan," responded
Groop.
"Hear me out at the very least, if you are not
comfortable with the plan then so be it," suggested
Floop.
Floop inquired about the ground layout in detail.
Groop did his best to explain, the *ins and outs*. Floop
proposed his plan to Groop quietly and secretly.

VI

The following day, on the eve of the *'Great Race'* and Sena's marriage to King Iso. Naut entered the mound that Sena and the Princess were held captive. Naut brought all two Anart seamstresses to measure a wedding dress for Sena.

Sena and Princess Shamora were discussing the times of the Groundies prior to all this misfortune when they were interrupted by Naut.

"Good day to you, soon to be *third Queen Sena*," said Floop "I have come to you by order of King Iso to have your gown made for the royal wedding tomorrow, all the Anarts and Groundies will be present."

"I will not," hissed Sena.

"Now, now, be gracious, you are not a servant," snarled Naut, "your boyfriend Floop will be racing tomorrow on the Ratz, one must not disappoint."

"Floop, racing,' said a relieved Sena, "besides, he's not my boyfriend, we're just very good friends."

"I would never have guessed, you two seem so close" retorted Naut.

The Anart seamstress attempted to measure Sena whilst the conversation continued between Naut and Sena. Princess Shamora sat quietly on her bed, she knew all too well the pain that Sena would be feeling. Naut stared at Sena he had an uncomfortable yet delightful feeling come over him. Sena noticed, call it women's intuition, she could sense Naut had been attracted to her. Sena decided to use it to her advantage.

"Do you have a girlfriend," asked Sena flirtatiously.

Naut is taken aback responded, "Me? No… no, don't
have the time, busy, busy, royal duties to carry out."
"I don't see why not?" said Sena.
Naut started to blush, the antennas on his head flopped
down, totally lame. Naut tried to wipe them away from
his eyes.
"Those eyes," said Sena noticing the flushed Naut,
"why is that such a good looking Anart such as
yourself should not a have wife."
"We cannot be talking like this, you are to marry the
King," responded Naut.
"If only things were different, given different
circumstances, me you, never-mind,' said Sena
suggestively.
"Go on," requested Naut excited.
"Well, I sort of find you very attractive," said Sena.
"You do!" exclaimed Naut.
"But none of that now, I am to be married tomorrow,
but if only you won the race," suggested Sena
Thoughts raced in Nauts' mind, he could win the race
then maybe King Iso would allow him to marry Sena.
That would be brilliant he thought. Princess Shamora
started to eavesdrop on the conversation.
"Maybe if you won the race, I could request that I
marry you," said Sena with a smile.
Naut could not contain himself, he paced up and down
the floors of the mound, mumbling to himself. Sena
remembered the potions she had taken from Wisen but
was taken away. The potions perfectly labelled with
descriptions *'Delirium'* - to make one delirious. *'Dew'*
- to create smog. *'Splinter'* - to make one run fast.
'Lotus' - to make one smell sweet. *'Flignog'* - to
make one smell terrible.
"I can make sure you win," said Sena.

"How to tell me, tell me?" yelled Naut.

"It must be our little secret, you know the bag your guards took from me when we arrived," said Sena.

"Yes!"

"In that bag, I have a secret potion that can make you faster than any other racer, nobody would stand a chance against you," said Sena "wouldn't you want to win?"

"Of course I want to win, wait let me fetch them," replied Naut excitedly.

Naut raced out and returned just as fast as he had left, he had the bag with him and instructed the seamstress to leave. Sena opened the bag, all was in order. She gently placed them on the table in front of Naut. Sena explained the purpose of each potion to Naut and them to him freely keeping behind the 'Lotus' and Flignog'. Sena made sure to repeat herself, "now remember carefully, at the beginning of the race, you give your Ratz the *'Splinter'* potion, that will make your Ratz faster than any other Ratz and their riders, you give the *'Delirium'* potion to the rest of the Ratz. As you about to finish the race, smash the *'Dew'* on the ground, that would create smog-creating confusion and my dear Naut will emerge from the smog as the winner and take me as the prize."

Naut nodded his head in agreement. Surely this will give him the advantage, he thought to himself.

"Now do not forget the plan, said Sena sweetly.

"I won't!" responded Naut, "I shall now take my leave, see you….tomorrow love."

Naut proceeded to leave. As soon as he was out of sight Sena shivered, her body in disgust.

"Do you know what you doing?" asked Princess Shamora.

"I don't know if it will work, but it's worth a try," responded Sena, "now if only I could get word to Floop."

Princess Shamora explained to Sena that on the day the *'Big Race'* all the riders will proceed to pass the Kings Podium for a final meet and greet. I would have an opportunity to wish the riders well even though the race is very biased. I suppose you being the next Queen of King Iso, it would be customary for the riders to meet you as well. This would give you the opportunity to talk to the riders especially Floop. Remember it is a very brief conversation, so Princess Shamora suggested Sena choose her words wisely. There was a sombre mood within the mound.

Naut had been extremely busy running from mud pillar to mud post, *love-smitten* as well, that he had completely forgotten to pick up King Iso's majestic gown from the fitters. He rushed to fitters to obtain the gown. The gown was cumbersome to carry, Naut held it with both hands swaying backwards and forward as he made his way to King Iso's personal dressing chamber. King Iso was not present in his personal chambers. Naut decided to hang the gown from two rods that protruded through the mud wall. Nothing more or nothing less was on Nauts' mind except for winning the race and taking Sena as his beautiful wife. Naut proceeded towards the conference hall to brief King Iso on the final preparations. As he entered, King Iso was at the end of the long table. Other Anart soldiers were present.

King Iso looked at Naut unmoving, "Can I perhaps help you with anything Naut?" demanded the King.

Naut cleared his throat and answered, "I have come to give the great King a briefing on the *'Big Race'* tomorrow."

King Iso gestured with his hands for Naut to join him at the end of the table. Naut proceeded to join King Iso nervously at the end of the table.

King Iso addressed the rest of the soldiers, "you see dear Anarts," pointing to Naut. "This is what you call a loyal Anart, does what is required and gets the task done, that is expected from all of you."

"Just doing my loyal duty to the King," said Naut.

"We all expect him to win the *'Big Race'* tomorrow and that he shall," retorted King Iso, "you see the Groundies or Carpils, whatever they call themselves; have dared come into my kingdom and tried to *hoodwink* me, I am much smarter than them and given that they have strayed into my Kingdom a lesson would now be taught!"

King Iso lay the drawn-out map that was confiscated from Floop and Sena upon their arrival. Laid it on the table in view of the Anart soldiers. In barged an enormous fierce looking Anart, hefty, muscular built in size he that stood about two and a half inches tall. A hideous sly smile adorned his grotesque face. Tiny skulls hung around his neck. A weighty broad sword hung from his hip.

"Pardon me, dear King, I had some unruly Groundies that need taking care of," said the enormous Anart.

King Iso shook his head and responded, "Zoof my trusted general, you're just in time, I was about to explain your next mission."

Zoof placed his hefty broad sword on the table,
THUMP! The table shook with its weight. King Iso
briefed the Anart soldiers on the two young Groundies
(Floop and Sena) and how they entered the Kingdom.
He continued to explain his brilliant plan to capture the
rest of Groundies that lived behind the Green under the
carpet and return them as slaves. King Iso handed the
map to Zoof.

"**Zoof,** you and the rest of the Anart soldiers shall enter
the lands and bring rest of the Groundies or Carpils to
me just before I wed that young, *yucky* Groundie Sena,
that would surely show my adversaries, that I am the
only King," instructed King Iso.

"Considered it done!' Yelled a fearless Zoof.

"And Zoof if any disobey, exterminate them by any
means," instructed King Iso.

Zoof lifted his sword of the table, placed it back onto
his hip and left the conference hall with the rest of the
Anart soldiers following.

Naut had decided that it was also his cue to leave and
proceeded to exit.

"Where are you going Naut?" yelled the King, "come
back here I would want a word or two with you."

Naut swirled around and proceeded to the long table,
he sat down on one of the mud chairs close the King.

"This is between us, my loyal Naut," said the King, "I
remember there as a time when I was your age; full of
youth and determination, you remind me a lot of
myself. I need you once the race is complete and the
marriage ritual concluded between myself and Sena."

"What is it that you need?' asked Floop. "I am at your
service."

"I need you to murder the newly crowned Sena in
front of everyone," instructed the King.

"Why?" asked a nervous Naut.

"You see my dear Naut, as I stated before, I don't have a need for her, the marriage is just for show," said the King, "I need to show the Groundies that by killing a nearly crowned Queen, that if they ever decide to oppose me or my authority I can massacre all of them, fear.. you put fear into the Groundies."

King Iso carefully laid out the plan to Naut.

Word spread amongst all the Anarts that King Iso would be marrying a third wife. Groundies were ordered to attend with the exception of the Groundies within the Dungeon. There was confusion amongst the Anarts as to why King Iso would be taking a third wife and all the Groundies were expected to attend as they had never been allowed at the *'Big Race'* before. *Chitchat* amongst the Groundies was spreading fast, another Groundie, named Pooples had received word that all the Groundies were allowed to attend the races. Pooples an activist slave, around the age of sixty-five, on many occasions tried to convince the Groundies to overthrow the Anarts and King Iso. Though to his disappointment in many attempts failed to convince the Groundies. Maybe this was the ideal opportunity. In this last-ditch attempt, Pooples decided to rally a few Groundies and discussed his plan. Many disagreed, though a few thought it would be a splendid idea and suggested Pooples address the crowd when the guards switch shifts. It was a very secretive meeting that would take place just above one of the mounds.

Pooples, dressed in rags, long wavy hair and a short beard stood in the middle of the crowd.

Pooples addressed a small crowd that had gathered, ***"I cannot bear the discontent much longer, and for thirty-seven years we trenched, dug and built the mounds for King Iso and his Anarts. Our sweat and tears drenched in every grain of sand. For far too long we have been slaves, the good old days just a blurred memory. I say we stand up, fight back, and take back what once belonged to us!"***

"How do we do that?" replied a Groundie.

"This is the first we are allowed to the ***'Big Race'***, I suggest we use this opportunity wisely," said Pooples.

"We won't stand a chance, they're too strong and too many," yelled another Groundie in the crowd.

"That is all in our mindset, we tend to fear whatever is bigger than us. We need to think smarter than them, we are Groundies after-all," said Pooples, "we shall strike when they least expect it!"

"What happens to us," said another Groundie from the crowd.

"I personally do not know what will happen, we may lose lives. Victory may not be ours, but we Groundies shall rather die trying than giving up!" professed Pooples.

"Then what's the plan?" asked an interested Groundie.

"Tomorrow on the day of the ***'Big Race'***, I will create a diversion by running onto the race field, during the commotion, you Groundies break down the walls, and escape" suggested Pooples.

The Anart guards returned; all the Groundies dispersed in separate directions.

VII

The Carpils were well on the way towards the Green, each Carpil carrying upon their backs as much that could be lugged. It was decided to travel on foot. It was a long tedious walk, they were approaching the edge of the forbidden land. They decided to take rest for the night. All the Carpils were exhausted, however, with hope in their hearts found the strength to keep going. King Mosesha suggested they should have a feast before entering the forbidden land. Male Carpils foraged around for delicious treats, they found long slimy worms, a few rare caterpillars and slugs. Ladies and young Carpils brewed *stick-beer*, handing them out to thirsty Carpils. There was a sense of peace shrouded by thoughts of apprehension. The male Carpils decided to cook the tasty treats that they so proudly caught. Songs were sung whilst children ran around playing. King Mosesha sat on a nearby rock and watched with deep satisfaction, he imagined to himself how delightful it is in the Green. Slew in the distance heard some commotion and decided to investigate himself what the disturbance was. As soon as Slew entered the group an unexpected cup of *stick-beer* was handed to Slew. He sat down on the floor and quietly listened to songs. Slew knew too well the days of the Green. He once had a wife and children, unfortunately, his wife and children were lost during the laying of carpet. It was nostalgic to many of the Carpils that were over the age of fifty-two. Some Carpils sat up a long table with chairs made out of old matchboxes. Neatly laying one next to other.

The food was almost done, all types of delicious meals were cooking away. *Slimy oozee worm stew, caterpillar rings, succulent slug broth.* Petunia decided to join the cooking furore and made a bright *pink slug stew.* King Mosesha instructed Uni not to stand guard and enjoy in the festivities. The meals were laid on the table and most of Carpils sat on the cardboard chairs next to the table, there wasn't enough space for all the Carpils. The younger Carpils and children decided to sit on the floor close to the table, close enough to listen to the stories being told. King Mosesha sat at the very end of the matchstick table. Laughter filled the dining area. Food flowed freely and Carpils ate to their heart's content. King Mosesha enjoyed his caterpillar rings in the usual ways, sucking hard around the rings trying to ferret out the hidden slimy nit-bits.

The meal had been polished and all the Carpils leaned back upon their chairs enjoying their *stick-beer.* One of the children requested a story of the Groundies. King Mosesha requested Petunia entertain the children with the story of the three brothers. Petunia gladly accepted. The rest of the Carpils were also keen to listen to the story. Silence fell upon the dining area, Slew also decided to sit closer and listen.

"Come closer children," said Petunia, *"let me tell you the story of the three Groundie brothers. Many many years ago, a king from a far-off kingdom had reached the age of two hundred and eleven, on his next birthday he would be turning two hundred and twelve and we all know what happens when a Groundie turns two hundred and twelve?"*

"The light fades away," yelled one of the children.

"Exactly," responded Petunia, *"now this Groundie King had three sons, named, Ziggly the oldest, Zag the middle, and Zog the youngest. Obviously the oldest, Ziggly would be the next King but the Groundie King decided it only fair that the worthiest of the three brothers should be the next King. The three Groundie brothers, Ziggly, Zag and Zog were all called by the King. The Groundie king explained to the three brothers that only the worthy would be the next King. Ziggly the oldest and most arrogant of the brothers thought it was unfair and that he should be the next King. The Groundie King proclaimed it and so, therefore, Ziggly had no choice but to accept it. The king requested that all three brothers venture deep into the lands and bring back one item, only one item. The brother that brings back the correct item would be the next successor to the King. All three brothers left in separate directions, Ziggly travelled North, Zag travelled East and Zog South.*

All three brothers travelled far and wide, across dangerous terrain. Eight months had passed and the Groundie King was getting worried as his twelve hundred and twelfth birthday was soon approaching. The kind decided to give them more time. On the ninth month, Ziggly returned with an item and wanted to eagerly show it for the Groundie King so that he may be given the kingship before his two younger brothers returned. The Groundie King advised Ziggly to keep it safe and only present to him once the other two brothers returned. Patience was definitely one of Ziggly's virtues. On the tenth month, Zag returned with his item and also wanted to present it to the Groundie King. The same was advised to Zag that he should wait until the youngest brother Zog returned. The eleventh month had passed and there was no sign of Zog, the Groundie King was getting worried that something may have happened to Zog. Time passed slowly towards the Groundie Kings two hundred and twelfth birthday, yet there was still no sign of Zog. The Groundie King had no other option to but to summon Ziggly and Zag to present the items. Ziggly very eager decided to present his item first. Ziggly explained that he travelled throughout the lands in the far North and searched for the best item. Ziggly presented the Groundie King with a dazzling sparkling white diamond. Zag explained how he travelled to the West up to the hills and mountains facing terrible danger. Zag presented the Groundie King with a bright gold nugget. The Groundie King had to make a decision as Zog had not returned as yet and time was running out. The Groundie king had no option but to proclaim his successor and the new King.

Zog ran in, just in the nick of time. The Groundie King asked Zog to present his item, Zog did not have an item. The Groundie King requested an explanation, Zog stated that he travelled to the far South, deep and wide but could find an item. Time was running out realised that he should return before the Kings two hundred and twelfth birthday. Zog apologized for not bringing back any item and stated that he would instead be close to his dear father the Groundie King before King's light faded. The Groundie King stated; Ziggly and Zag I thank you for the effort but I have no need for any diamonds or nuggets where I am going. The best item or gift you could ever give me is that all three of you, brothers are with me till the end. I will, therefore, have one successor, but three, all three of you, the kingdom shall be split up into three separate kingdoms. Ziggly, Zag and Zog to rule each Kingdom alongside each other. With that, The Groundie King's light faded out."

All the children and the rest of Carpils clapped and cheered. King Mosesha suggested that they have all have a good night's rest for tomorrow they will all venture through the forbidden lands towards the **'GREEN.'**

The guards in the dungeon delivered the usual disgusting food to the prisoners within the mud cells. Floop looked at the bowl of the blob. He hadn't eaten a single morsel since being held captive within the cold, crummy dungeon. His stomach twisted with knots within knots, almost trying to digest its self. Floop decided that in order to win the race, he would require some nourishment. Staring at the yucky thick blob, Floop grabbed some of the *blob food* with his hands rolling it into a ball. With his mouth wide open, shoved it down and swallowed it without chewing. Roll after roll he made, swallowing in disgust, often gurgling to avoid throwing up.

"You get used to," said Groop, "you just have to imagine it as being a good grub, only a little imagination is needed."

Floop in-between swallowing responded, "I have tasted disgusting food before but this is purely loathsome."

Floop decided to get a good night's rest, he lay his weary head upon the awkward mud bed, staring through a hole high up the mound he could make out a star, the *Sirius* star, the brightest star that glowed in its gleaming blue hue. He wondered what Sena may be doing.

Sena sat upon a fine chair staring out through the holes in the mounds at the sky, she too looked at the *Sirius* star at the exact time… Floop lay staring at it from with his mud dungeon cell. A warm feeling passed through Sena's body.

Sena sang in her sweet melodic voice,
"Sight, sounds, have no fear, for tomorrow,
Brings a new day, a new sunrise, a new song,
Let your beauty shine tonight, for tomorrow will
come,
And you will still be here, I wish upon your bright
light,
That I may see you again. Tomorrow, tomorrow is
not that far away,
Tomorrow holds a new day, a new sunrise, a new
song for us to sing,
We dance and sing beneath your beauty as you watch
upon us from way, way up there.
I wish that I still may see you tomorrow."

Within the midst of the forbidden land, marched the four brave warriors, Stix, Stones, Rok and Hardes. Mist and smog filled the air, a tense feeling taken with every step. Within the darkness, they crept. Long struts of dry weed lay across the path. Brown thick moss grew in all different directions, sidewards, downwards, upwards, moss growing over other moss. The stench changed with every step. Rok and Stones and swung their words, slashing through the dry weeds clearing the path. A stream of water flowed alongside the wall. The warriors decided to fill their water flasks and rest for a while. Rok heard a few rustles and promptly investigated. It was a just a few stink beetles bustling around. Rok snatched them up and returned to the rest of the warriors neatly seated on pebbles. Stix brewed some *stink-beetle ale* and with the rest of the insides of the beetle, prepared a *beetle insides stew*. The *stink-beetle ale* warmly welcomed as it touched their drenched lips. They all sat on pebbles talking about the days that have gone by. Stones recalled of the days when his father would teach him and Stix the fine art of archery. The bow had to be strung from the finest string and the arrows straight as a pin. Archery may seem easy, but takes years of practice and patience. Archery is a skill of using bows to shoot arrows. Stix and Stones (identical twins, Stix with black hair and Stones with white hair) father had died when they were young, during an electric explosion within the Carpil village, he had mistakenly switched the wires positive on positive and negative on negative terminals of the damaged batteries that had fallen through the carpet. Stix, Stones, Rok and Hardes were all about the same age mid-thirties and all of them been born a Carpil, they all have never seen the "Green' so they too had no knowledge of what to expect. Rok and Hardes best friends from the time they were young lads, played sword fighting amongst each other during every opportunity they got. With each strike of swords against each other, so too did they develop a unique skill. They collected the silver coins and that fell through the carpet and with the assistance of the blacksmith smelted themselves the finest edged swords. King Mosesha brought the four of them together as the Carpil village huntsmen. They weren't warriors, however, with their specialised skill of weaponry they ought to have been. The need for warriors was not a concern for the Carpils, until now.

Wisen and Diggles, rode upon their roaches deep with the forbidden land, Diggles jiggling up and down groaning with pain and discomfort. The area much deeper and wider lay sprawled with growths of spiky dry twigs. The area barren from any water, dried twigs and grainy sand, hungered for a drop of water. Dangers lurked around them. Hungry beastly eyes could be felt watching them. Diggles and Wisen's roaches were scared too, however, pushed forward. Abruptly, Wisen stopped.

He was now facing a *furry toothed, pink tailed beast* fuming at him. Wisen locked his eyes with the furry beasts blood red eyes. Slowly descending from the roach still keeping his eyes locked, the furry beast stopped fuming and stared directly into Wisen's eyes. Diggles had stopped too and descended from his roach ever so quietly. Eye to eye, Wisen and the furry beast stared at each other. Neither blinked. Wisen slowly stepped backwards still keeping eye contact. The beast tried gesturing forward to attack but stopped when Wisen stopped. Piercing relentless eyes fixed on each other. Wisen taking each step slowly backwards until there was enough space between the furry beast and himself. He swiftly raised his walking pin and struck the sharp pointy end into one of the furry beast's eyeballs. The furry beast squealed in pain. Much angered, the furry beast scratched on the grains of sand creating a cloud of dust.
Wisen grabbed Diggles by the arm and screamed,
"Run you buffoon, Run!"
The dust cloud cleared behind Diggles and Wisen as they ran, they could hear the screeching of the roaches as the furry creatures devoured on them.
Wisen and Diggles were now on foot as they walked through the dense forbidden land with no weaponry of defence, Wisen relied on Diggles to guide them to the wall, it was a big ask; however, Diggles gladly pointed the way forward admirably.

The time had arrived for the four warriors to continue on their path towards the *'Green'*. Stix and Stones sharpened the tips of their arrows, Hardes found a rock to sharpen his sword, as he swiped his sword on the rock back and forth sparks flew followed by ear-wrenching sounds with every swipe. Rok studied the map.

"Should not be far now," said Rok.

"What did you say?" asked Hardes.

"Stop sharpening your sword, and listen you *numb-skull*!" yelled an annoyed Rok.

"Don't call me a *numb-skull*, you *bone-head*," responded Hardes.

"I so wish to see the green, with my own two eyes," said Stones, "had always been my dream to one day walk in freedom, to have the fresh air blow in the face."

Stones suggested they all form a pact and placed his hand stretched out, Stix, Rok and Hardes all stretched out their hands, placing it on top of each other.

"Brothers till the end!" they all yelled in unison.

They were all well on the way, there was no sign of any furry, toothy, long pink tailed beasts that Diggles had so aptly warned them about. The path seemed to be mostly overgrown with dry weeds. Hardes enjoyed swiping at the weeds, the sound of weeds breaking satisfied him greatly. They travelled forward along the wall as instructed. A flag protruded from the ground, they all stooped to the words written, ***'Sena alone, headed towards the green.'***

"The young Sena travels," said Stones, "what could have happened to her?"

"What happened to young Floop?" asked Stix.

They all stared at the flag, wondering of the circumstances that may have befallen the young Carpils. Stones wrote below the flag, *'Stix, Stones, Rok and Hardes all four, headed forward'*. Placed it back in the ground. They all bowed their heads in honour of Floop. There was silence as they walked along the path that Sena had recently passed on her own, they could see her fresh footprints on the ground. They could hear ruffling in the thick moss as they walked along, though no beast or creature attacked them. It seemed as all will be fine. There was a foul smell that lingered in the air, not the usual stench but a tangy sour smell that they could almost taste. They ignored the smell and continued on their journey…the smell disappeared and the normal stench of the air returned. Then the foul smell returned and disappeared. It was in repetition over the next few steps, the foul smell would return and disappear. It was becoming unbearable. The foul smell getting even more pungent as they progressed further, it smelt like old damp rotting worms.

"What is that awful, putrid, ghastly smell?" yelled Rok.

"You smell it too?" asked Stones, "I thought I was going crazy."

There were giggles coming from the front of them, Hardes trying his best to keep in his laughter, swishing at the dry twigs.

"Is that you?" asked Stix. "Is it you Hardes, that is passing that stench from your bottom."

Hardes could no longer contain himself and burst into a belching fit of laughter. He was laughing so hard that the foul smell was passing freely from his bottom.

"Yuck!" shouted Rok, "did something die in your stomach?"

Hardes responded between laughter, "I need to take a poop!"

"Well, could you not have done this earlier?" yelled Stix.

"I didn't feel like I needed to at the time," answered Hardes.

They all stopped and started to slap Hardes. Now even more smelly gas expelled from Hardes bottom. Stix, Stones and Rok were all trying to hold back on gag reflexes. Though Stix did eventually vomit all over the ground.

"Go, go no, and go take a poop!" yelled Rok.

Hardes found a quiet place next to a stream of water, some distance away from the rest and relieved himself. He had cleaned himself, as he was doing up his pants he was knocked over his feet. Standing up to his feet dazed, an old untidy, long-bearded Carpil tried in vain to take refuge behind Hardes.

"It's after me!" yelled the old Carpil.

"What is after you?" yelled back a confused Hardes.

"That furry beast, look, look!" yelled the old Carpil.

A furry, toothed beast rushed towards Hardes. Calmly he reached for his sword from his waist, just as the furry beast approached snorting and scratching its feet against the ground, Hardes swiped at the furry beast across the throat. The furry beast slumped down with a **Thud!** Stix, Stones and Rok upon hearing the commotion, quickly ran to the aid of Hardes. The furry beast lay dead on the ground. They all examined the furry beast, as this was the first time they laid eyes on such a creature. The old Carpil slowly manoeuvred his way from behind Hardes and also stared at the furry beast.

"You got him good you did," said the old Carpil.

"Yeah, I did, easily!" bragged Hardes.

"Wait, who are you?" requested Hardes.

Stix, Stones, Rok and Hardes now fully focused on the old untidy looking Carpil.

"Well it is I, Shroom," replied the old Carpil.

"Shroom, is that really you?" asked Stones in astonishment, "we all thought you were a goner, whatever happened to you?"

Stix suggested it best to find a place further away, besides the awful smell of the furry beast, Hardes waste matter could also be smelt. All four warriors including Shroom walked towards an isolated, still smelly but better smelling area against the wall. Shroom tried to hug the four warriors, they were not the hugging type. Shroom flimsily sat on a pebble, wobbling from side to side until he had reached some stability. Stix, Stones, Rok and Hardes also sat on pebbles leaning against the wall. They all eagerly awaited Shrooms' story…

"Well get on with it then," insisted Rok.

Shroom bowed his head and spoke, *"I have walked a lonely path, and the time had stopped for me. I have not a single clue to the time I have spent, walking in my own shadow. Chasing after something that does not exist. With no purpose, I roam this forsaken forbidden land. For far too long I have lived in the darkness, my being consumed by nothingness. I am empty, often closing my eyes to sleep I drift off to happier times when the land that was once ours. When I dream my feet lift off the ground and I fly, soaring over all the free Carpils. I wished not to wake, my desire to forget is not possible. Foraging on the scraps of half-eaten bug carcases. But you know my life was never like this, there was a time I was young you know, I had a beautiful wife, Oy! Sena, my little Sena, my loving granddaughter, that hypnotic innocent smile and eyes, I miss those little fingers and how she would run screaming into my arms, I would swing her around and she would laugh, how she loved to laugh. I miss those days. Those little moments, they aren't little. Alas, it is but a distant memory, I cannot return, my mind is lost, drifting from reality to dream. The shame and embarrassment I have bestowed upon my Sena and my dear wife. Sometimes it is best not knowing, living obliviously. The heart shattered into many tiny pieces. My destiny is such that I may perish within this forbidden land. Where darkness sleeps, forgotten!"*

Stones wiped a tear from his face, for he too experienced the pain of losing his father at a very young age. He would also dream of a far-off land, where he and his father together with Stix would go hunting in open wide fields with no roof above, running freely over hill tops in deep green pastures. Stones pulled his emotions together.

"Do I have news for you," said Stones.

"I would prefer not knowing, my life bells have rung," replied Shroom.

"I would rather show you," said Stones.

Stones led Shroom to the flag that had been placed earlier upright. Shroom read the flag, ***'Sena alone, headed towards the green. Stix, Stones, Rok and Hardes all four, headed forward'***. Shroom looked in horror, his face turned pale, his eyes swelled up, tears flowed down his cheeks, a trail of dirt from his cheeks followed. He fell to his knees.

"What have I done?" cried Shroom.

"Stand up, you're here now, be the man you once were," said Stones, "there is always *hope*!"

Stones sat alone with Shroom and gave him a full account on the circumstances that had come to pass to the present and bring to his attention that the Green had been found. He also went on to explain that Sena is now a young sprightly fifteen year old, and Petunia had gone slightly *whoopsy*. Stones suggested Shroom join in the brotherhood that the four warriors had earlier formed.

"So shall it be!" exclaimed Shroom. Stones out of his normal character gave Shroom a warm embracing hug.

Four warriors, now became five as they made their way towards the 'Green'. Hardes from the font continued clearing the thick twigs with huge swipes with his sword. Rok had decided to join Hardes swiping as well. They were getting further and further away from the Carpil village, there were no thoughts of ever going back, and it was now a distant memory to all. Stix, Stones and Shroom lagged behind, Shroom talked and talked, he had not spoken to anyone in seven years but Stix and Stones did not mind. Shroom often jumped in excitement retelling tales he had encountered in the forbidden land. Stones found the tales very amusing and often laughed. Hardes had made his last vicious swipe at the twigs, and there it was a hole in the wall. The 'Green'. They all slowly moved towards the edge of the hole and stared at the magnificence of the 'Green'. There was a feeling of amelioration.

Stones suggested they rest and make their way tomorrow into the long-forgotten land of the **'GREEN'**. Stix did the usual and foraged for food. At the edge of the hole of the wall the opening of the window to the Green, Stix found some wild berries growing and hurriedly plucked them. Shroom the oldest and the only one with the knowledge of life on the Green decided he is best to prepare them. For the first time...Stix, Stones, Rok and Hardes tasted fresh plantation. They were all *gob-smacked* in the delicious, sweet scrumptious juices that exploded in their mouths. A feeling of sheer ecstasy, each mouthful bursting with more flavour. Stones requested a second helping and slowly nibbled on each berry. Twirling and swirling it around in his mouth, making sure to get all the juices sprawled across his mouth. Stones sat down and stared into the Green. He thought to himself of how proud his father would have been of them all. A sight that would be permanently stained in his memory. Rok suggested they take rest with each rotating sleep so that one of them be keeping an eye out for any unwanted trouble. Stix and Stones sat higher up on the top of high growth of moss. Rok, Hardes and Shroom sat further below. Hardes suggested he stays awake first whilst the rest of them sleep. Hardes sat at the edge of the hole leading to the Green, he watched as night started to fill, the sun had already dipped its tired head and in its place, a bright white full moon appeared. It was a clear night with bright stars neatly stuck on a perfectly woven black blanket. He was fully enraptured in beauty. Perfection.
"Charge!" yelled Zoof.
It was an ambush! Lead by Zoof with hundreds of Anart soldiers, spears in hand charged at Hardes.

"We're under attack!" shouted Hardes.

The Anart soldiers were streaming in, swiping their spears at Hardes, Rok and Shroom. Rok and Hardes swiped fiercely back at the Anart soldiers, clashing of swords and spears at each other. Stix and Stones from above the high moss growth pulled their bows from their shoulders and shot at the soldiers. Hardes sliced and swiped his sword through the soldiers as they fell. From his head he twisted and swung his sword across the soldiers, Rok thrust his sword into soldiers, swiping through as many as he could.

"They are too many!" yelled Rok.

"Keep going," Hardes yelled back.

Zoof in his huge attire briskly walked towards Shroom, lifted him full off the ground and flung him into the wall. Hardes rushed over to Shrooms assistance. Zoof pulled out his huge sword from behind his back and swiped a full thrust towards Hardes. Hardes moved swiftly to the side as Zoof's sword came swishing pass him. There was blow after blow from Zoof's sword, Hardes fell backwards but managed to lift himself up. Harder swings of the sword came towards Hardes as be blocked them with his sword. Swing for swing Hardes and Zoof exchanged blows towards each other, Rok was surrounded by soldiers as he swiped and thrust his sword into them. Stones instructed Stix to continue shooting bows from the top of the moss and hurriedly ran in assistance to Rok. Stones lifted two of the spears from the ground of the fallen soldiers, one in each hand and he pierced it into the soldiers. A soldier almost struck Rok from the back, Stix from above moss shot an arrow right through the body of the soldier and into another soldier.

"Keep going!" yelled Stones, thrusting his spears into soldier after soldier.

Wisen and Diggles had heard a commotion and decided to follow the sounds.

Thrust for thrust, swipe for swipe, Zoof and Hardes exchanged hard blows towards each other. With a huge hard swipe, Zoof struck Hardes sword out of his hands.

"You will die!' shouted Zoof.

Zoof lifted his heavy sword up towards his waist and prepared himself to thrust it towards Hardes. Shroom gave a huge bite with all his might into Zoof's ankle, Zoof looked down at Shroom and kicked him airborne into the thick moss. Stix noticed an impending end to Hardes.

"Stones, Hardes needs help!" yelled Stix.

Stones ran towards Hardes and Zoof, as he approached Zoof turned around and plunged his sword into Stones, slowly pulling it out. Stones froze, blood seeped from the open wound from his chest.

"NO!" screamed Stix.

Stix lifted his bow, took aim and shot an arrow directly into Zoof's shoulder, piercing the shoulder with the point of the arrow protruding out.

"Ahhhhh!" screamed Zoof, "retreat, retreat." All the Anart soldiers followed Zoof as they fled into the Green.

Wisen and Diggles, arrived just as the Anarts fled. Stix ran hurriedly towards Stones, grabbing him as he fell back against the ground. Stix held onto Stones' hand as he wept.

"No, no, stay with me brother, hold on, you hear me, hold on," yelled a weeping Stix.

Blood seeped slowly through the open wound staining Stones long white hair. Rok, Hardes, Shroom, Wisen and Diggles stood over Stones.

Stones spoke between difficult breathes, *"Let it be, I walked my road, I have seen the Green with my own eyes, I am now free brother!"*

Stones struggling lifted his own arm around Stix head and pulled his forehead towards his. Closed his eyes and slumped, the light faded from Stones. Everyone laid down their weapons and bowed their heads.

In the dark of night, a moment of silence followed as Stones lay on the ground lifeless. Wisen suggested Stones be given a worthy burial in the Green. Hardes and Rok found an open piece of the area on the Green. They dug into the Green as a sad moon looked down upon them. They did not expect their first steps onto the Green to be so mournful. Stix quietly sat in a corner of the wall, they all thought it best to give Stix some personal space. Shroom greeted Wisen and Diggles. The mood around was sombre. Wisen stood in deep thought as he watched as Rok and Hardes dug deeper into the ground. Diggles and Shroom stood talking amongst themselves. Rok and Hardes emerged from beneath the pit that they had just dug. Diggles, Shroom, Rok and Hardes lifted up Stones body and carried it into the Green and placed it gently into the neatly dug grave. All took turns in covering the grave with the remaining sand. Stix and Wisen walked to the foot of the grave. Stix requested if Wisen would be kind enough to say a few words. Wisen folded his arms in respect.

"Today we have lost a friend, a brother, Stones a brave warrior till the very end," said Wisen, "I think he would not want his life to go in vain. We are Carpils and we should celebrate his life, for tomorrow is a new day for all of us, we must not forget there is and will always be hope, within the darkest times, we should always hold onto hope. We have made it this far, with hope in our hearts, let's go reclaim our home."

Rok and Hardes said a few closing words. Wisen advised them that the rest of the Carpils are on foot behind them.

Once four warriors, then five, now six. Stix, Rok, Hardes, Shroom, Diggles and Wisen awaited daybreak.

VIII

The day had arrived for the **'Big Race'**. The land filled with various activities, the Anarts looked forward to this day every month as they were allowed the day-off. The races held every month allowed King Iso to address his soldiers and workers. It was more of a day of flamboyance from King Iso, showing his great power. He would stand in front of all the Anarts within the enclosed walls of the colossus stadium, giving them long speeches about how great he was. Of course, there was only one winner of all races, which was Naut. Predictable at every race. The race would have twelve riders, six of the best Anart riders and six Groundie riders racing on the backs of Ratz. The Ratz were well trained and fed well, they had a special compound especially built to house the Ratz. The excitement and amusement with Anarts came through the demise of the Groundies, often during a race, some of Groundie riders would be severely injured and even killed. The races were very dangerous, the Anart riders were allowed to carry a weapon whilst the Groundies were unarmed. Groop, the best Groundie rider's life was spared as it brought the race to a climatic end. There was always a great celebration post-race. Naut would be carried around the stadium as a hero whilst stones and mud bricks were thrown at the other Groundie riders. Groop would be taken quietly through the back entrance back to the dungeon, where he would await the next race. A worthy race opponent for Naut.

Often Groundie slaves who were thought to have deserved punishment for disobedience were brought to the centre of the stadium and whipped by Anart soldiers. The Anarts would cheer, often screaming for the death of the Groundies. On special occasions, there would be a battle between Zoof and several weak Groundies, with Zoof showing off his strength by killing one Groundie at a time. Whenever Zoof battled in the stadium he would call on others to verse him, none dared to, Zoof showed no mercy. Groundies were never allowed to attend the *'Big Race'* as spectators. Today would be different, the Groundies were not invited but allowed to watch the wedding ceremony of King Iso to Sena.

A new rider had been added to the race, Floop a Groundie from a distant land. The Groundies upon hearing the news passed on whispers to each other. Questions were being asked, who was he? Where did he come from? Were they to be excited? All types of questions were being passed around the Groundies. Sena's name also mentioned, the bride to be. The Groundies were growing tired, the torment the torture, hope had slowly dissipated from the hearts of the Groundies. Most Groundies longed for the sweet call of death. Hope turned into despair, blackening their hearts with hatred for the Anarts.

Sena awoke to the sound of hustling Groundie servants within the mound. She peered through the holes of the mound, Anarts were busy below the mound in precise formations, carrying out various activities. Sena noticed Princess Shamora seated on one of the chairs deep in thought. Sena thought to herself that it may be best not to disturb the Princess and continued watching the below activities. She was soon disturbed by the seamstress that barged in, holding a white wedding gown in hand. The seamstress promptly pulled Sena up and dressed her in the gown. Pulling and tugging at the gown to get the perfect fit. The gown didn't fit as well as expected, the seamstress annoyed undressed Sena and left the room to make the last minute adjustments to the wedding gown. Sena felt violated. Princess Shamora had a good laugh.

"You find this all amusing, don't you," retorted Sena.

"It is your special day, is it not," teased Princess Shamora.

"This is not what I imagined my wedding to be," said Sena, sitting down followed by huffing.

"Life sometimes isn't fair dear Sena but we take what life dishes out to us and try and make the best of it," responded Princess Shamora, *"sometimes we eagerly await for change, but it does not come, most perish in despair for trying was never an option for them, you see Sena, there are circumstances beyond our control, we can either accept our fate or change it, it takes a lot of bravery, but choice depends on whether to fight back or not."*

"So then, why do choose to be locked up?" asked Sena.

"Good question," answered Princess Shamora, "I never did give up, circumstances are for now, besides I made a choice with me staying here and providing King Iso with the youth potion, I am merely buying time for the other Groundies."

"Can you reverse the ageing process of the youth potion?" asked an intrigued Sena.

"I would not dare, King Iso would slaughter all the Groundies including myself,' responded Princess, "whatever you thinking, forget it!"

 Sena persuaded Princess Shamora to make a youth potion with the reverse effects, an *advancing-age* potion. Princess Shamora took much persuasion but eventually made one dose of the age advancing potion and handed it to Sena.

Princess Shamora suggested she apply some beauty make-up for Sena. That also took a lot of persuasion from Princess Shamora for Sena to agree. Sena sat upon a chair whilst Princess Shamora did her make-up also deciding to curl Sena's long luscious black hair.

The *colossus stadium* slowly started to fill up. It was
an oval structure made out of mud and grey stones to
reinforce the building. It was grey with hints of brown
colour. Multiple layers of seating adorned the oval
shape, giving it a unique appearance. At the one end of
the structure where the two oval walls joined, sat a
massive seating for King Iso and his Queen. At the
opposite end stood an announcement stand. There
were small mud sound tubes built around the stadium
whereby, when the time was needed for King Iso to
address the crowd, he would speak into the tubes. The
sound would travel between tubes and out of small
openings for all to hear. The announcer on the
opposite end would also use these sound tubes to make
the necessary announcements. There were many
entrances for the Anart spectators to enter and exit.
Secret passage tunnels were built from various mounds
leading to the stadium. King Iso had one of his very
private passage tunnels built for him to enter and exit
the stadium. Some tunnels led directly from the
dungeons to the stadium. There was also a special
tunnel built for the entrance of the Ratz. Within the
centre of the stadium, stood another oval open area
with barriers. This area was dedicated to battles that
Zoof proudly participated in. Around the smaller oval,
lie a huge race track. The centre of the stadium this
time had been specifically decorated for the wedding
to take place in full view of Anarts and Groundies.
Anart workers were busy setting the final
arrangements in anticipation of the wedding. This time
a separate entrance and exit was allocated for the
Groundies.

King Iso stood in his private chambers, lifting up his heavy majestic robe, it was a woolly, long black robe with thicker woollen white edges. He placed it around his body and clipped the two ends around his neck. His crown sat nearby on a cushion. He had earlier summoned Zoof as he heard he had returned. King Iso was very eager to receive the news of success from Zoof. There was a knock on the private chamber doors.

"Come in," yelled King Iso.

Zoof entered the room, by now he removed the arrow from his shoulder that Stix had shot at him. We walked towards King Iso and bowed down.

What news have you got?" demanded King Iso.

Zoof remained bowed and answered, "King, we have been to the edge of the land, there we found only four Groundies."

King Iso requested Zoof stand up, Zoof stood up, however, kept a distance away from King Iso.

"I see you have been injured," said King Iso.

"A mere scratch,' responded Zoof, "There were not many, I managed to kill one of them, easily."

"And the rest!" yelled the King.

"I don't think they will be providing any trouble, scared they were," answered Zoof, "I would think they would return back to where they came from."

"Do not think!" yelled King Iso, "I have sent you on one task and you have failed me!"

"No, dear King," answered a shaken Zoof.

"Mmmmm," said the king stroking his chin in thought, "I do not think we should take any chances, make sure there are soldiers stationed outside the stadium."

"As you wish," responded Zoof exiting the King's private chambers.

"And Zoof, do not let me down, this is a very important day," said the King.

Zoof left the King's private chambers and shut the door behind him. There was another knock on the door.

"Now what do want?" screamed the King.

From behind the door came a response from one of the guards, "it is us, we have come to escort you to the stadium."

King Iso requested the guards enter the chamber.

"Is the stadium filled?" asked King Iso.

"Yes, great King Iso," answered one of the guards, "Anarts and Groundies have filled the stadium, they await your great presence."

"Send for the bride and Queen Shamora, I want them seated beside me. Queen Shamora to my right and the bride to be on my left, what is the bride's name?" requested King Iso

"Sena, her name is Sena," replied a guard.

King Iso lifted his crown from the cushion and placed it upon his head. On the table lay a small dagger, King Iso picked up the dagger and placed it behind his back in his belt. The guards formed a formation around King Iso and proceeded to exit the chamber towards the long tunnels that would lead to a private entrance into the stadium.

Sena and Princess Shamora were being dressed by the seamstress when a group of guards entered the mound.

"Are you done as yet," yelled a guard.

"Show some respect you nitwit, remember I am still your Queen and Sena will soon be your Queen as well!" yelled Princess Shamora.

"You will never be our Queens," retorted the guard, "we serve under the great King Iso, so I shall respect your title and not yourself."

Princess Shamora thought it best not to argue and requested the same from Sena. The wedding gown fit snuggly on Sena, long white in colour with shiny silver seams sewn through the gown. With full make-up and curled hair that touched her shoulders. Sena was surely a sight to behold.

"The stadium is filled to capacity, the expectation is that you are seated before King Iso arrives," said the guard, "the correct protocol needs to be adhered to, and you shall both stand when King Iso arrives, bow to him and take your seats, Queen Shamora on the right and Sena you on the left."

"I will not bow," insisted Sena.

Princess Shamora advised Sena it would be best to follow the protocol. Also reminding Sena that the riders would also be introduced to them. Sena stubbornly agreed. Sena placed the small bottle of *age-advancing* potion within her leather undergarment, neatly tucked out of view. Sena sprinkled the *'Lotus'* (to make one smell sweet) potion on herself. Princess Shamora and Sena followed the guards through the tunnels to the secret entrance of the stadium.

The announcer yelled through the sound tubing, "May I introduce your Queen Shamora and bride to be Sena."

Sena and Princess stepped onto the royal podium, the stadium was packed with Anarts and Groundies. There were cheers and screams from the Anarts. The Groundies that were present sat at an isolated area of the stadium quietly. Wave to the crowd suggested Princess Shamora to Sena. Though very hesitant Sena waved to the crowd and sat down leaving a space between them for King Iso.

"We want the King, we want the king!" yelled the Anarts.

"Calm down, he is on his way!" yelled the announcer through the sound tubes.

King Iso stood at the entrance of the stadium, dusting his gown and straightening his crown.

"How do I look?" King Iso asked one of the guards.

"Magnificent as usual Sire." responded the guard.

"Here is your King Iso!" yelled the announcer.

King Iso entered the stadium welcomed by cheers and shouts from the Anarts. King Iso walked up to the edge of the royal podium in full view of all the Anarts and Groundies. He stood proudly and patiently waiting for the shouts to subside before he spoke. The shouts slowly subsided and turned to silence as they waited for King Iso to speak. King Iso did not need to use the sound tubes as his voice was loud and deep enough for all to hear.

"My dear Anarts and you disgusting Groundies," said King Iso garishly, *"today we not only have the 'Big Race' but I will also take a third wife, another Groundie. We have found two young Groundies that dared venture into my Kingdom, it is only just that we show you Groundies that I am the only King within these lands. By marrying the girl, it will ensure that you Groundies know your place and if you ever thought that there would be hope, you are sadly mistaken. There is no Hope! I am the only King and all you Groundies shall comply and embrace me just like the rest of the Anarts. The other young Groundies will ride in the races and will lose as expected. I am the only King, there can only be one!"*

The Anarts all cheered and booed at the Groundies seated in the Stadium. Pooples seated at the edge of the stadium could feel his blood boil, he wanted to run into the field and strike at King Iso.

Wait, the time will come," said a Groundie pulling Pooples back into his seat.

"I cannot take this any longer," retorted Pooples.

"Patience, let's watch and wait, we are all with you, daring as it may seem, we're with you," assured the Groundie.

The announcer requested a female Anart to sing whilst the Ratz and riders were prepared to enter the stadium.

The female Anart stood behind the sound tubes and sang,
"Oh King of Kings, so dear, so great;
The greatest King of them yet.
The one who conquers all with might;
We serve to you in honour and pride.
From all Kings deep to all Kings low;
No finer King than the one we know.
May the sounds of fear fill the hearts of those;
Who challenges you as their foe.
We are all too faithful to our King,
Trust and loyalty we shall bring.
Live and rule forever, our King;
The greatest of all. O, King of Kings."

Floop and Groop had finished changing into their leather riding gear and awaited the guards. Floop had already made up his mind that he will win the race irrelevant of the warnings that Groop had given him. Groop sat upon his mud bed and requested Floop sit next to him.

"You know Floop, after all these years I have never had a friend," said Groop, "I am and will forever be grateful for your friendship, Many Groundies do not make it back alive, so if anything happens to me please know that…"

"Nothing is going to happen to you," responded a reassuring Floop, "we ride together, I have never ridden in a race before, and so I will follow your lead."

"Keep your head and chin up, they're filthy cheating Anarts they are," responded Groop, "try and ride as close to me as possible."

The guards arrived and unlocked the gates.

"They're ready for you," said the obnoxious guard,
"let's get going."
Floop and Groop followed the guards through the
dungeon, there were still Groundies tied against the
walls.
"Win! Win for us!" yelled one of the Groundies tied to
a wall, the guard struck the Groundie with his spear.
Floop and Groop stood at the entrance to the stadium
behind another four Groundie riders. The other six
Anart riders including Naut stood further in front
waiting to be introduced to the crowd, King Iso, Sena
and Queen Shamora. There were twelve riders in total.
"As you eagerly awaited, here are the riders!" yelled
the announcer.
The first six Anart riders with Naut at the end were
ushered onto the royal podium in full view of all, the
procession was as follows, firstly they would be
greeted by Queen Shamora, the King Iso and lastly
Sena. They would then turn, line-up and face the
crowd. The same would apply to the six Groundie
riders. The five Anart riders followed lastly by Naut,
were ushered to meet the Queen, King and Sena in that
order, Queen Shamora shook the rider's hands, then
King Iso graciously gave those taps on their shoulders,
Sena refused to shake the hands of the Anart riders,
King Iso snubbed Sena and instructed her to shake
their hands, Sena did so unwillingly.
"The champion rider Naut!" yelled the announcer.
Naut welcomed by cheers from the Anart attendees,
Queen Shamora shook Nauts hand and wished him
well, King Iso hugged Naut.
Remember our plan," whispered King Iso.
Naut proceeded to Sena as she shook his hand she
winked at him flirtatiously.

"You need to win," whispered Sena.

The six Anart riders lined up in front of the crowd.

The Anarts cheered whilst the Groundies sat quietly.

It was time for the Groundie rider to be introduced, the first four Groundie riders walked pass Queen Shamora as she shook their hand and wished them well. They passed King Iso as he ignored them, they proceeded to Sena as she warmly hugged them. Groop entered, Queen Shamora shook his hand and wished him well.

"I hope you win this one," said Queen Shamora.

King Iso too ignored Groop as he passed, Sena warmly hugged Groop.

"You have a good Groundie, look after him," whispered Groop.

Floop entered, there was *booing* from the Anarts spectators. Floop walked towards Queen Shamora, she lifted her hand and gently touched Floop's cheek. King Iso too ignored Floop as he walked past. *Floop's mouth opened in awe as he looked at Sena dressed so beautifully, his eyes fixated on the sheer beauty of Sena*, he had not seen her like this before. Sena hugged Floop.

"You, you, look and smell so…," said awe struck Floop.

"*Shooo now*, you making me blush," whispered a shy Sena, "remember this carefully, Naut is going to give the **'Delirium'** potion to Groundie Ratz, it is important that during the race to switch to one of the Anart Ratz."

King Iso harshly pulled the two apart.

"This is not a reunion, get on with it you filthy Groundies," said King Iso.

The remaining six Groundie riders lined up and faced the crowd, The Anarts booed whilst the Groundies cheered. There was an exchange of vile words between the Anart and Groundie spectators. The twelve riders, six Anart riders and six Groundie riders were escorted to the starting line to meet their Ratz.

VIIII

The Ratz were held by their trainers, they stood five inches high by six inches wide, a brown leather harness around its chest and neck. A saddle placed on its back, a leather mouth guard placed around its face, followed by two black straps for the riders. Only the senior and best trainers were allowed to train the six Anart Ratz for the Anart riders. The inexperienced and younger trainers were allowed to train the Groundie Ratz. For ease of names, the six Anart Ratz names were Ratz 1, Ratz 2, Ratz 3, Ratz 4, Ratz 5 and Ratz 6. Naut had the honour of always riding Ratz 1. The rest of the Ratz that were allocated to Groundies were Ratz 7, Ratz 8, Ratz 9, Ratz 10, Ratz 11 and Ratz 12. None of the Groundie riders was specifically assigned a particular Ratz. They had to mount any of the available Ratz from 7 to 12. Usually, Groop chose Ratz 12. Naut was allowed to inspect all the Ratz as he was the reigning champion.

Naut carefully reached for the potions Sena had given to him, three in total *'Dew'* (to create smog), and *'Delirium'* (to make one delirious) and *'Splinter'* (to run faster). *'Dew'*, he kept tucked in a pouch behind to his belt. While nobody watched, Naut inspected the Ratz, gave Ratz 1, his personal Ratz the *'Splinter'* potion, he did not give the splinter potion to the other Anart Ratz. He gave the *'Delirium'* potion to the Groundie Ratz 7 to 12. All the riders were requested to mount their Ratz. **Naut climbed on to Ratz 1** and the rest followed. Floop immediately recognised the Ratz as the furry toothy, long-tailed beast he had encountered in the forbidden land. **Groop climbed onto Ratz 12** as usual. There was only one Ratz available, Ratz 7. **Floop mounted Ratz 7** and remembered what Sena had whispered to him earlier. All the Ratz, with their riders firmly mounted, were escorted by their trainers to the starting line. The spectators cheered, The Anarts for the Anart riders and the Groundies for the Groundie riders. The race was about to start. There was no specific number of laps around the stadium, it was the rule that the only rider that finishes the race alone, is declared the winner.

King Iso stood up and raised his hand, all the Ratz were now jerking and pulling as the Riders tried to keep them sturdy. King Iso dropped his hand. The riders strapped the Ratz and all rushed forward leaving a massive cloud of dust behind. Each rider strapping harder and harder at the Ratz to go faster. Ratz 2 and Ratz 8 slammed into each other flinging the riders into mid-air. The race continued each rider for themselves. They passed the first bend and then the second bend with great momentum. Naut had taken the lead after the first lap and was in full velocity. An Anart rider on Ratz 3, rammed into Ratz 10, a Groundie rider, leaving the Groundie to tumble on the ground. Another Anart Rider on Ratz 4, kicked the Groundie rider full in the face as he passed. The *'Delirium'* on the Ratz was starting to kick in, Floop started losing pace and slipped to the back of the pack. Groop on Ratz 12 gained some pace and was closing into Naut on Ratz 1 when his *'Delirium'* potion also started to kick in. Groop started to slip back. An Anart rider on Ratz 5, passing Groop, tried to kick him but missed and tumbled to the ground. Three laps had passed and Naut was still ahead of the pack. The *'Delirium'* started to affect all the Groundie Ratz. A Groundie on Ratz 11, smashed into the spectator wall, Anart Riders rode over the Groundie as he lay motionless. Groop had slipped back, side to side with Floop.
"You need to switch your Ratz!" yelled Floop.
Five laps had passed, Naut passed Floop and Groop.
"Told you, I am the winner," mocked Naut.
An Anart rider on Ratz 3, passed Floop and was about to pass Groop.
"Get ready," yelled Floop.

As Ratz 3 rode alongside Groop, trying to slam into him, Groop jumped onto Ratz 3 and flung the Anart rider off. ***Groop was now riding on Ratz 3,*** riding hard and strong. A Groundie on Ratz 9 got wedged against the wall by an Anart rider on Ratz 4, both riders hurling to the ground. Groop was gaining on Naut. As Groop passed an Anart rider on Ratz 6, the Anart rider attempted to hurl himself at Groop and missed falling to the ground. His Ratz 6 was still running without a rider. Groop rode up to Floop stretching out his hand.

"Grab onto my hand!" yelled Groop.

Floop did as requested and held tightly onto Groop's back.

"When I pass Ratz 6, jump on it," said Groop.

As Groop passed Ratz 6 still without a rider, Floop daringly jumped onto Ratz 6 and pulled on its straps. There were only three riders left in the race, ***Naut firmly in the front on Ratz 1, Groop on Ratz 3 and Floop on Ratz 6.*** The Anart and Groundie spectators were standing on their feet screaming and cheering. All three riders, Naut, Groop and Floop were riding with sheer gait. Thirteen laps had passed and all three riders within inches apart from each other. Naut eager to win the race at any cost pulled out the ***'Splinter'*** potion, leaned forward and shoved it into his Ratz's mouth. It did not take long before the ***'Splinter'*** potion started to work on Nauts Ratz again. It blitzed forward in full acceleration, leaving Groop and Floop far behind. Naut was headed for victory and all he had on his mind was Sena and taking her as his bride as the winners' prize. King Iso would surely agree he thought to himself. Lost in thought, Naut lost control of the fast Ratz 1 and slammed into the stadium wall just at the Kings podium. Naut slumped flat face into the ground. The Anart crowd, booed whilst the Groundies all cheered. Floop and Groop slowly approached the Kings podium, pulled at the straps of the Ratz, bringing them to a halt, they both dismounted their Ratz.

The Anart spectators picked anything they could find on the floor and flung it Floop and Groop. The Groundie spectators clapped and cheered.

"Groundies, Groundies," they all screamed in unison.

A disappointed King Iso stood up and addressed the crowd.

"SILENCE!" yelled King Iso, "We all know the rules there can only be one winner and as I see it, nobody has won!"

All the spectators went silent. Floop and Groop stood on the ground looking up at King Iso on his royal podium. King Iso continued, "We need a winner, I proclaim that the race is not over until there is only one left standing. I propose that these two Groundies battle each other till death!"

The Anarts all cheered.

"We will not fight!" yelled Groop, "Those days are over."

King Iso pulled Queen Shamora towards himself, pulled out the dagger from behind his back and held it firmly against Queen Shamora's throat.

"Well if you don't fight, I will kill your dear Princess Shamora!" shouted King Iso.

"Don't!" screamed Princess Shamora.

"Okay, wait, let me talk to the Groundie," responded Groop.

Groop suggested to Floop they battle each other, Floop flatly disagreed.

"I do not see the point," said Floop, "the King will have us killed anyway."

"Exactly," replied Groop, "this way at least one will have a fighting chance, I suggest you kill me."

"Never, I will not," retorted Floop.

"Listen to me, I have lived…." said Groop turning to face the podium, ***"we will battle!"***

"Good, and make it a worthy fight," replied King Iso, "Throw them some swords."

Two swords were flung into the Arena, Groop proceeded to pick them up and handed one of the swords to Floop. Groop swirled the sword around to get a feel of it. Floop with no prior battle or weaponry experience held the sword awkwardly with both hands. Groop struck the sword at Floop missing him on purpose.

"I do not know how to fight," said a frightened Floop.

"Just raise your sword as I strike," replied Groop, "let us give them a show."

Groop lifted his sword and struck at Floop as he raised his sword to block, knocking the sword out of Floop's hands. Groop walked over to Floop's sword that lay on the ground, using his own sword, flipped the sword up from the ground and handed it back to Floop.

"Keep your hands sturdy and tight around the handles," advised Groop, "let's try this again."

Groop swirled his sword around his back giving a show to the audience, allowing enough time for Floop to obtain a good handle on the sword. Groop attacked Floop again, this time Floop holding firmly onto the sword.

"That is it you doing it," said Groop, "just keeping going."

Groop struck at Floop several times, each blow from Groop's sword Floop blocked. The silent Anart spectators started to cheer. Groop continued striking at Floop as he blocked every strike. The strikes from Groop's sword started getting harder and harder. Floop could feel his hands starting to throb.

"It is no use!" yelled Floop.

The battle became one-sided and very boring, this infuriated King Iso and the Anart spectators. King Iso summoned Zoof to enter the Arena. Zoof ran and jumped from the top of the podium landing on his feet followed by a puff of sand from his feet. Zoof wasted no time in attacking Groop, swipe after swipe at each other. Floop looked on and tried swaying his sword loosely at Zoof, completely missing and stumbling with the weight of the sword. The battle between Zoof and Groop intensified. Groop with his feeble sword against the might of Zoof and his hefty sword. Swing after swing, clashing steel and sparks flew as the swords met each other. Floop stood in dismay, he could not do anything but watch as the battle started to get more intense.

"It is time to go," said a Groundie in the crowd to Pooples, "they're going to kill him.

Pooples jumped off the barrier and ran towards the brutal battle taking place, he swiftly grabbed Floop's sword off of his hands. Pooples twirled the sword and entered the battle taking place between Groop and Zoof.

"Some more meat!" yelled Zoof, "Let's see what you can do."

Pooples and Groop stood side by side as Zoof swung his enormous sword at theirs. Pooples swung around to avoid the sword as it whisked past him.

"Come on Groundies, let's bring this building down!" yelled a Groundie in the crowd.

The spectator Groundies starting hitting firmly at the colossus stadium walls, using the loose plummeting rocks, struck them into the thick walls.

Zoof lifted his sword above his head and with great might swung down at Groop's sword, on impact splitting Groop's sword in two. Groop stumbled and fell to his back on the floor facing Zoof as he stood over Groop. **Zoof lifted his hefty sword and struck it deep into Groop's abdomen, twisting the sword, followed by a crunch sound.** Pooples from behind Zoof jumped into the air and with his sword landed it into Zoof's shoulder. Zoof turned around with Pooples sword still dangling from his shoulder in a nonchalant manner, yanked out the sword from Groop, blood dripped from the sword as it was pulled out. He struck at Pooples with all his might, Pooples dived away from the callous swings from Zoof. The colossus stadium started to shake as it started to crumble down. "Take cover!" Yelled on the Anarts in the crowd. There was a big *THUD!* The walls of the stadium caved in. Pooples quickly dived at Floop as a massive lump of mud fell towards Floop.

From the king's podium scram an embittered King Iso, **"FIGHT!"**

King Iso grabbed Princess Shamora and escaped deep into the secret tunnels below the stadium. Naut followed behind them.

"Groop!" screamed Floop reaching out his hands, with Pooples pulling him to safety as the walls tumbled down.

"He's gone!" Pooples yelled back.

All the Groundies rushed into the arena, Zoof pulled out the dangling sword from his shoulder and swung at the rushing Groundies. Zoof swung fast and hard at the storming Groundies. Slicing through them. The Anart soldiers and Anart spectators stormed the arena and joined in the battle. Groundies against Anarts. They ferociously attached each other. The Anarts that fell, the Groundies quickly picked up their spears and used it as weaponry against the Anarts. Sena from above the podium, ripped off her wedding gown, beneath it revealing her leather pants and vest. She quickly descended from the podium to the arena floor, lifting up spears that were scattered and accurately flung them at the Anarts.

"We need to fight," said Pooples to Floop handing him a sword.

With new found courage and animosity, Floop firmly grabbed the sword from Pooples hand and swung at the Anarts with deep resentment flowing through his veins. Zoof swung deep and hard into the hearts of the Groundies, leaving their bodies mercilessly scattered on the ground.

"Surround them!" yelled Zoof to the Anarts.

The Anarts formed a circle around the Groundies, leaving them vulnerable. The Groundies now faced the inevitable they were defeated and all be slaughtered. Pooples raised his sword within the circle of defenceless Groundies.

"We fight, no matter what the outcome may be, we are no longer slaves, stand firm and fight with all your might, for we are Groundies!" professed Pooples in loud audible words.

The Groundies formed a circle around themselves with the Anarts surrounding them in an outer ring formation, their spears all pointing forward towards the Groundies. Zoof entered the circle. Pooples approached his sword in hand, ready to attack.
"Do you think this Groundies have any chance against us great Anarts, they are mere slaves and that's all they will be, let me show you how it is done!" yelled Zoof. Zoof lifted his sword high above his head. Floop standing directly in front of him holding his sword in both hands. Zoof took a deep enormous breathe and with all his might brought his sword down towards a brave Pooples. **Midway Zoof stopped, a long thin arrow, protruded out of his chest. Zoof looked down at the arrow and dropped to his knees, gurgling and fell to the ground.** The Groundies stood aghast and stared at the source of the shooter, in the distance from on top of the fallen rubble of the colossus stadium, stood Stix bow in hand.

Bringing up to the rear of the Anarts, Hardes and Rok
struck ruthlessly into the Anarts with their swords.
Swinging with precision swipes, cutting deep into the
Anarts strike force. Groundies joined in the onslaught
of the Anarts. Each one falling to the wrath of the
Groundies strikes. Floop, Sena and Pooples fully
armed and striking at the Anarts with sheer fortitude.
"Retreat to the tunnels!" yelled an Anart soldier.
The few Anarts left standing hastily hurried towards
the tunnels.
The dust slowly settled against a backdrop of anguish.
Brave Groundies lay injured and dead sprawled on the
floor. Wisen and Diggles approached the arena,
looking at the devastation that had now come to pass.
Groundies rushed to their loved ones, some alive,
some not so fortunate. Tears flowed and cries
followed. Anarts soldiers lay motionless on the
ground. Taking in the blanket of darkness, walked in a
barrage of Carpils. Lead by King Mosesha, Petunia,
Slew, and Uni all the Carpils arrived at their utopia
only to find ruination spread across the land. Older
Carpils immediately recognizing their long lost friends
and relatives ran to each with warm affection,
embracing each other. Petunia's once pink face turned
pale white as she stared at the man in front of her.
"Is it you," asked Petunia.
"Yes it is I," answered Shroom.
Petunia grabbed hold tightly of Shroom, tears of joy
flowed from her pale cheeks. Petunia did not want to
let go of Shroom. Next to Petunia now stood a docile
Sena, Petunia grabbed hold of Sena and pulled her into
the hug. Slew fell to his knees, he had never thought of
the day that he was allowed to see such a sight again.
"Pooples!" yelled Slew in hesitance.

Pooples, still walking around the desolation, halted to the familiar voice, turned around and strained his eyes to focus on the person shouting his name. Pooples ran with all his strength, hugging Slew with all his might. "Dad!" wailed an emotional Pooples.
It was a reunion draped in painful sorrow. The courageous motionless Groundie bodies that lay sprawled, were quickly counted and moved to a temporary place of decency. Some Groundies sat and some stood around the rubble of the once colossus stadium. Heads bowed in respect for the fallen. King Mosesha overheard a few Groundies talking about the bravery of Princess Shamora. King Mosesha's eyes filled with joy and searched desperately around for signs of Princess Shamora his daughter.
"Floop, have you seen Princess Shamora?" asked King Mosesha in desperation, Floop bowed his head.
"King Iso has taken her," answered Floop.
"Taken her where," demanded King Mosesha.
"Deep into the tunnels," said Floop, "he's taken her with him."
"We must find her at once!" retorted King Mosesha.

Floop humbly bowed to King Mosesha and rushed to
Pooples, interrupting the family reunion with Slew.
They both entered the tunnels and searched, there were
many tunnels, Pooples and Floop decided it would
best to split up. Tunnel after tunnel they searched.
Pooples reached the chamber where King Iso's second
wife, the Queen of the Anarts' sat. He promptly set her
free without asking any questions and suggested she
flee to safety and never return. Floop searched and
searched in vain. There was no sign of Princess
Shamora, he ran to King Iso's private chambers that
too was empty. Floop had remembered the Groundies
locked in the dungeon, rushed promptly to set them
free. There were screams of joy as the gates of the
dungeon doors flung open. Floop and Pooples met
within a central chamber, both nodded in
disappointment. They both dreaded the walk back to
inform King Mosesha that there was no sign of his
dear daughter, Princess Shamora.

Floop and Pooples were about to deliver sorrowful
news to King Mosesha when an unanticipated King
Iso emerged from one of the nearby mounds, holding
the dagger firmly against Princess Shamora's side.
Naut and a few Anarts emerged from the mount as
well. King Iso firmly holding the dagger to Princess
Shamora's side walked towards the gathered
Groundies.
"This is not over!" yelled King Iso, **"I want the long-
life potion!"**
King Mosesha stepped forward still keeping a fair
distance away.
"Give us the Princess,' shouted King Mosesha, "I will
gladly give you the potion."

144

"How can I trust you?" screamed King Iso.

"It is ours to give, I will give it freely, just release the Princess," begged King Mosesha.

"No, throw me the potion and I will release this turd!" yelled King Iso.

Sena ran to join King Mosesha, pulled out a small bottle of potion from her leather vest and waved it King Iso.

"Here, I have it!" shouted Sena, "I will trade you me for Princess Shamora, and I know how to make the potion, plenty of it."

Floop attempted to run towards Sena, Pooples held him back.

"Noooo!" screamed Floop.

"Okay, you have a deal," said King Iso, "walk slowly towards me… slowly."

Sena looked back at Floop and the other Groundies as they lowered their heads. Sena slowly walked towards King Iso, from behind her she could hear Floop squealing with Pooples to let him go.

"Okay, I am here,' said Sena holding onto the potion, "Me for Princess Shamora that was the deal."

King Iso reached forward and grabbed Sena, pulling her towards him, allowing Princess Shamora to break free of his tight grip. Princess Shamora ran into King Mosesha's arms as he embraced her.

"I now have the potion!" yelled King Iso, grabbing it out of Sena's hands and gulping it down.

It did not take long for the effects of the potion to kick in, **King Iso, started to squirm, twist and contort his body in agony. Long strains of Grey hair and beard started growing from his head, his torso crumpling up.**

"You tricked me," yelled an old feeble King Iso.

Sena had kept her side of the deal with King Iso, she gave him the potion but the potion was the *'advancing-age potion'* that Princess Shamora had given her earlier. Naut rushed to King Iso's aid, remembering that he had still in his possession the **'Dew'** potion (creates smog), that Sena gave to him. He lifted up the potion and slammed it onto the floor. A huge cloud of smog immediately filled the air. Sena heard a voice faint whisper from Naut, "I will be back my love."

The thick blanket of smog cleared, there stood Sena alone. King Iso, Naut and the rest of the Anarts disappeared. Pooples released Floop as he ran with great elation towards Sena. Sena welcomed Floop with a warm tight embrace. Sena cupped Floop's face in her hands and gently and ever so lovingly kissed Floop on the cheek.
"Promise me one thing you nitwit," said Sena.
"Anything," responded Floop.
"Never leave my side again!" requested Sena.
All the Groundies including the lost Carpils joined in a celebration to celebrate the life of another departed Groundie. King Mosesha climbed up a heap of rubble with Princess Shamora by his side to address the now silent crowd eagerly awaiting King Mosesha's speech.

"Dear fellow Groundies and Carpils, I am two hundred and eight years old, I have lived and seen many faces of my dear friends and family pass into the light. We all know the bitter taste of despair and hopelessness. Many lives were lost, we must not forget to celebrate their lives and the sacrifices they made. Dark nights too many shrouded by the unknown. We all dreamed of a new day, a day when we all can roam freely, young and old in any shape or size. That day is today my dear Friends. We are all Groundies including the Carpils, we are one family. As long as there is hope in our hearts, with pure thought and good intentions, nobody can defeat us. In our darkest moments never let go of HOPE!"

All the Groundies cheered. Wisen walked up to King Mosesha and unwrapped the item he so carefully kept by his side. Pulling away from the cloth, emerged a sturdy shiny gold crown with red rubies encrusted around the edges. Wisen lifted the crown for all to see, the Groundies clapped their hands in excitement. Wisen lifted the crown to place upon King Mosesha's head. King Mosesha courteously took the crown from Wisen's hands.

"As I mentioned before," said King Mosesha, *"I am an old man now and wish to rest my weary eyes, and tired limbs, it is time for a new leader, someone much younger and wiser."*

King Mosesha walked towards Princess Shamora and placed the crown firmly upon her head and bowed. All the Groundies followed suit and graciously bowed to the new Queen Shamora. Princess Shamora now the rightful *Queen of the Groundies*!

About the Author

M.D Ley was born in Johannesburg, South Africa, in the early eighties to a middle-class family. He was the youngest of three children, a late lamb. Raised by a strict father a teacher by profession and a loving ever forgiving mother. Through M.D Leys youth he played in the dust and sand, kicking soccer balls and excelling on track and field obtaining provincial colours for 100m and 200m sprints respectively. Mischievous by nature, he found himself in hot water most of his youth and was often blamed for the wrong doings of other kids in his circle. Labelled the mischief maker, he soon grew fond' of the whippings which were freely dished out by disillusioned parents. At the age of thirteen, M.D Ley took up various small jobs to earn extra money, one of those being that of a 'paperboy'. He painstakingly saved up enough money to even support his parents during tough days. Information technology intrigued M.D Ley as he fiddled with computers. His curiosity served him well and his show of entrepreneurship glistened brightly as he began selling specially built computers for customers from the age of sixteen. Earning a decent living though not enough. His aspirations were far too high. After completing school, due to financial constraints and difficult times he could not pursue a University qualification full time. M.D Ley immediately started working at the age of eighteen for various Banks, learning and studying through these institutions and obtaining various qualifications in Finance.

Simultaneously, he studied part-time at a higher learning tertiary institution in Information Technology and Television Media obtaining various local and international qualifications.

Coming Soon:

ALITA and her fabulous thought machine

GROUNDIES
"Trilogy"

www.MDLey.com